JULES BENNETT

CLAIMED BY THE RANCHER

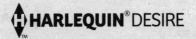

HARLEQUIN® DESIRE

Recycling programs
for this product may
not exist in your area.

ISBN-13: 978-0-373-83851-6

Claimed by the Rancher

Copyright © 2017 by Jules Bennett

Printed in U.S.A.

National bestselling author **Jules Bennett** has penned over forty contemporary romance novels. She lives in the Midwest with her high-school-sweetheart husband and their two kids. Jules can often be found on Twitter chatting with readers, and you can also connect with her via her website, julesbennett.com.

Books by Jules Bennett

Harlequin Desire

What the Prince Wants
A Royal Amnesia Scandal
Maid for a Magnate
His Secret Baby Bombshell

Mafia Moguls

Trapped with the Tycoon
From Friend to Fake Fiancé
Holiday Baby Scandal
The Heir's Unexpected Baby

The Rancher's Heirs

Twin Secrets
Claimed by the Rancher

Harlequin Special Edition

The St. Johns of Stonerock

Dr. Daddy's Perfect Christmas
The Fireman's Ready-Made Family
From Best Friend to Bride

Visit her Author Profile page at Harlequin.com, or julesbennett.com, for more titles.

To my plot angels for this story:
Elaine Spencer and Melissa Jeglinski.

One

The bell on the door to Painted Pansies chimed, and nerves danced in Pepper Manning's stomach. Opening a shop with her one-of-a-kind paintings and unique fresh floral bouquets had been on her bucket list for some time. She might be a drifter, a free spirit of sorts, but her creativity—her ability to make something from nothing—was what really drove her.

Coming back to Stone River, Texas, however, would take some master creative skills. She would certainly be making something from nothing—a business, a home to call her own. Pepper had always loved this town, so it made sense for her to make this the place where she started the next chapter in her life.

Besides, time was not on her side.

If she hadn't had anyone else to think about, she

could've chosen a different town to settle into, but in five short months, she'd be a mother.

A *single* mother with no one else to turn to for support.

Pasting a smile on her face, Pepper stepped through the doorway from the back room and her entire world came to a halt.

The man standing at the display of cheery tangerine roses had Pepper gripping the edge of the door frame. That profile, the black cowboy hat, those narrow hips she'd once known so well…

No. This was too soon. She needed more time. How could she be thrust into her past already? Though she'd been in town a month, this was her first day launching her brand-new business.

She'd assumed he most likely still lived in town because of his family's ranch and vast holdings, but she hadn't geared herself up to face him just yet.

Would she ever be ready to face the man who broke her heart at the most vulnerable time of her life? The man she'd been so certain she'd be spending her life with.

Before she could muster up some generic greeting, Nolan Elliott's gaze swept around the shop and then landed on her.

The flare in his eyes calmed her somewhat, as he was plainly just as stunned to see her as she was to see him. He quickly masked his emotions as he took a step toward her. She sighed despite herself. Apparently some things never changed.

"Pepper."

That low, sexy drawl of his hadn't changed over the years. He still managed to make her toes curl with that piercing blue gaze and those strong, broad shoulders. And that mouth. He'd done plenty to make her squirm with that mouth, too.

"I had no idea you were back in town."

Thankfully, the tall cash wrap separated them. Pepper stepped forward, leaning her hands against the edge. She needed a little support.

"I've been back about a month," she replied. Small talk, she could do that. "I took a few weeks to make this place my own, so this is my first official day open."

He glanced around again, and she hated how she waited to get his approval. She'd given up letting Nolan Elliott have any control of her mind or her heart years ago when she left town...or so she'd thought. Yet somewhere deep inside her lingered that young, naive girl who thought this man was her everything. She knew better now, but that didn't mean she couldn't appreciate how undeniably sexy he still was.

"This is a nice store. Good location, too."

The old two-story brick building had belonged to her grandparents decades ago. They'd never sold it and her free-spirited, nomadic parents had no interest in staying. Granted, she didn't necessarily want the building, either, but with her funds at an all-time low, she had no choice.

"I assume you're in need of flowers? Or were you here to look at the paintings?" she asked, hoping to move this process along because having Nolan this close, where she could see him, inhale all that tantalizing masculinity…it brought back an onslaught of feelings she just couldn't handle right now.

"Flowers," he replied easily, as if he wasn't torn up on the inside. Clearly the memories weren't threatening to strangle him like they were her. He'd pushed her away and obviously moved on without a second thought. "But this artwork is exceptional. I remember how much you loved painting."

He *should* remember because she'd tried to teach him…and that had ended up a disaster with paint all over them, which led to the best shower sex of her life. Well, the only shower sex, but regardless, the experience had been epic.

Nolan examined another canvas with bright flowers before bringing that heavy-lidded blue gaze back to her. He tipped up his black cowboy hat, a familiar move she'd seen him do countless times. Only he wasn't the same cowboy he'd been when she left. Now he was a big, broody, powerfully built man, hotter than she'd ever thought possible.

Being a member of the prestigious Elliott clan didn't hurt him, either. Gorgeous and wealthy were a lethal combination. He'd been both of those when she'd loved him before, but that had nothing to do with how fast and hard she'd fallen for him. He'd been so much more than her boyfriend, her lover. He'd been her very best friend and she'd thought her soul mate.

After she left, she'd wondered if it was all real, if her emotions were just those of a guileless young woman who hadn't any life experience yet. Unfortunately, she'd done too much thinking since she'd been gone.

Pepper wasn't sure what all he'd done in the past few years—she'd purposely distanced herself to keep the pain at bay. She did know that, despite his privileged upbringing, Nolan had wanted more out of life than ranching. He'd been determined to help others. And it was that damn career goal that had ultimately been the catalyst that ripped them apart.

Nolan's lifelong dream had wedged its way between them and had him choosing his unknown future over her. Over their family.

The Elliotts were one of the wealthiest families in Texas, probably the country. Pepper had loved their home on Pebblebrook Ranch. She'd once envisioned a life there, a life with Nolan and their baby. The two of them had even designed a home together and she'd thought for sure they'd live happily ever after surrounded by puppy dogs and rainbows. That was how naive she'd been, because she'd never once considered that something could rip them apart.

But something had and all of those dreams had been stripped away, leaving her with nothing but a shattered heart.

Nolan moved back to the display of roses, giving her a full visual of those tight jeans over slim hips. Pepper closed her eyes, took several deep, calming breaths and willed the memories to go away. She was trying to rebuild her life, not get swept up in the darkest moments of her past.

She'd known she'd come face-to-face with him eventually. Heck, she'd even played out the scene in her mind. But nothing had prepared her for the crushing reality of the actual moment.

"Roses are too typical for a first date."

Pepper swallowed. Of course he'd be shopping for a lady... Why else would a man come into her shop? And she wasn't stupid. Nolan was a very attractive man, a rich rancher to boot—what woman *wouldn't* want to go out with him?

Still, why did she have to be privy to his wooing tactics? That was just more salt in the wound that had never healed.

But she'd opened this business for a much-needed fresh start, and she needed it to be a success. Which meant she had to cater to all clientele so she could start making money. No matter who walked through her door.

Pepper pulled on her professional panties and squared her shoulders. "What type of lady is she? Does she have hobbies? That can tell me quite a bit about a person, if I know her interests."

And if this faceless woman had an interest in Nolan, Pepper already knew enough...and she hated her with a fiery passion.

Nolan turned toward her once again. "She works at the hospital with me. I'm not sure what she does outside of that."

Her heart hitched in her throat. So he had fulfilled that dream of becoming a doctor after all. He'd followed through and now had everything he'd ever wanted. Nolan was the type of man to never let any obstacle get in his way…no matter who he hurt in the process.

"I assumed you'd still be ranching at Pebblebrook." She hadn't meant to let that thought slip out.

"I help out when I can. That's definitely Colt's area of expertise." Nolan crossed his arms over that powerfully broad chest, and Pepper had to force her eyes to remain on his. "I'm a surgeon at Mercy Hospital, so my schedule can be crazy at times."

A cowboy and a doctor? Did he have to up that sex appeal by telling her this? No doubt this woman was a cute little perky nurse. She probably also had a perfect waistline and could fasten a pair of size-two jeans.

Drawing in a deep breath, Pepper smoothed her tank over her round abdomen. The most comfortable things for her these days were her long flowy skirts and her tanks. Anything that stretched along with her belly.

"Okay, then. Let's not do roses," she suggested. "What about a variety of colors in a bouquet? I have a few options over here with some tulips or some with daisies. Tulips are classy. Daisies are more fun."

She moved from behind the counter and started for the front of her shop. But she'd taken only a few steps when she heard Nolan's swift intake of breath.

That past she'd hoped to never face again had officially hit her square in the face.

Nolan prided himself on control and the ability to think on his feet and hide his emotions. For a rancher and skilled surgeon, there was no other way to live.

But seeing Pepper Manning with a baby bump had knocked the air right out of him…as if seeing her after ten years wasn't enough. She was still just as breathtaking as he remembered. Then again, their sizzling physical attraction and sexual compatibility had never been the issue.

No…those aspects of their relationship were beyond compare. He exhaled roughly, rubbing a hand across his stubbled jaw, as the memories assailed him. His fear of commitment at such a young age and the pregnancy and subsequent miscarriage were what had ultimately torn them apart. It had all been too much, too soon, and to say he hadn't handled things well would be a vast understatement.

But he'd been afraid. That fear had spawned his actions and he'd been too prideful to admit it. Ultimately, he'd let everything go in an attempt to save himself. He'd never forgiven himself, but he sure as hell didn't want to dredge up all of that now. He'd moved on, and it was obvious Pepper had, too.

Even so, having her so close yet being unable to reach out and touch her was difficult. She personified beauty, and she'd captured his heart once, so long ago…but he wasn't sure that man existed anymore. The miscarriage had broken something inside him that had never fully healed.

Pepper was clearly stronger than she'd been years ago. Her beauty was just one of the things he'd loved about her. Her inner strength was definitely another. But seeing her now, ready to move forward with a child, only proved she'd handled the situation better than he had.

She had always wanted a family; he'd always wanted to be a surgeon. Dreams they hadn't discussed because they'd been too caught up in the euphoric throes of young love. The type of love that naive couples felt could carry them through anything. Obviously that had turned out to be a bold-faced lie.

His eyes raked over her again from head to toe. How could she be just as stunning, just as vibrant, as ever? Her curves were still as alluring, her breasts fuller than before due to the pregnancy, and her long mahogany hair still hung like silk over her shoulders. His hands itched to feel those exquisitely soft strands gliding through his fingers.

Nolan cursed himself for allowing the past to rush up and assault him, but Pepper had always managed to wield control over him like no other woman before or since.

Now he couldn't help but wonder if there was a husband or significant other in the picture. Not that it was any of his concern, but…was there? Despite everything, he found himself wanting to know everything that had transpired since she'd left. He had zero rights to her life, but that didn't stop the intrigue from creeping in.

Pepper clasped her hands together just below her abdomen, the bangle bracelets jingling on her arms. She'd always had a thing for jewelry, he remembered fondly. Then her dark eyes suddenly held his as if she dared him to make a comment. Nolan hardened his jaw. He'd never backed down from a challenge before and he sure as hell wasn't going to let the unbidden memories overpower him now. He'd come too far, had everything he ever wanted. Every bit of angst that settled between them was from a different time, a different life.

He'd literally given up everything to be where he was today. There was no looking back, no time to dwell on the regrets that always seemed to be just below the surface.

"Congratulations," he said, offering her a tense smile.

For a fraction of a second, her eyes narrowed. But then she nodded. "Thank you."

Those memories might be from another chapter in their lives, but they'd left so much unresolved. He'd gotten angry, broken things off, she'd left town…and that was pretty much the end of it.

Stubborn male pride had kept him from searching for her, and with his money he could've hired anyone and found her in record time. But he hadn't. She'd left to get as far away from him as possible, and like a fool, he'd let her go.

They'd said some hurtful things after the miscarriage, things he continued to cringe over when he thought about them. But the damage had been done; they'd strayed too far from the blissfully in-love couple they'd once been.

Nolan didn't see a ring on her finger, but that didn't mean anything. Regardless of the fact he shouldn't care, he wanted to know more. He was just getting reacquainted with an old friend…that was all, he reassured himself.

Though at one time they'd been so much more.

"Where are you living now?" he asked casually.

"Upstairs, actually. It's a small apartment, but perfect for me, and it saves money."

Perfect for me. That told him all he needed to know about a man in her life. There wasn't one. Instant relief swept through him, which was hypocritical considering he was here to buy a gift for another woman.

Still, Pepper had a story and he wanted to know every detail.

No! No, he didn't. He was here to get flowers for his date and that was all. Then he would head home and catch some sleep. After a traumatic night in the OR, he needed to regroup. Maybe he'd take his favorite stallion out later for a ride so he could unwind and think.

His dinner date would certainly revive him. Nolan had asked this particular nurse out months ago, but their schedules had just now lined up.

"How far along are—"

"This bouquet would be perfect." She cut him off. Clearly, he was not welcome in her personal space. "There's a few peonies, roses and lisianthuses."

"I'll take it. Go ahead and pick out another bouquet."

Her dark brow quirked as she shot him a side glance. "For tomorrow's date?"

He bit back an oath. This unexpected reunion

needed to come to an end. No good could possibly come of it, no matter how irresistibly drawn he still was to this woman. Need he remind himself that *he* was the one who'd let her go? He'd thought at first that might have been a mistake, but over time, as he grew up, he'd realized it had been the right thing to do.

They had been ripped apart by grief and they wanted different things. He had no right to be carrying a torch for her after so long. Even if, in all honesty, seeing her pregnant hit him in a way he couldn't quite explain.

"Actually, Colt's fiancée's birthday is in two days."

Pepper's features softened at the mention of his baby brother. "Oh, sorry. I didn't mean—"

"It's fine." He reached forward, taking a premade pink vase with blooms of all sizes and colors. "She'd love this one."

Silence settled between them and Nolan couldn't pull his gaze away from hers. They were practically strangers now, but he knew those eyes. They'd always been so expressive and now was no different. He'd never met anyone else with eyes such a mesmerizing shade of dark gray. Pepper was definitely one of a kind.

Weariness reflected back at him now, though, and he couldn't help wondering what she was facing right now. She was alone, and that tidbit of information didn't sit well with him.

There were too many parallels to the last time he'd seen her, so it was impossible not to be swept up in nostalgia and bittersweet memories.

Pepper was all woman now, however. There was a level of maturity, almost an underlying stubbornness, that hadn't been there before. The defiant tilt of her chin, the rigid shoulders, as if she dared him to bring up the past. Fine by him. He was all for living in the here and now… He just hadn't expected to do it with her back in Stone River.

"I honestly didn't expect to see you this soon," she muttered. "It's harder than I thought."

Nolan swallowed…that guilt he'd been so good at tamping down suddenly threatening to overcome him.

"If this is too difficult—"

"No." She shook her head. "We've moved on. It's fine, just…different."

She pushed her dark, satiny hair back with her hand, those bangles jingling again as she pasted on a smile. "Is this all you need? Two bouquets?"

"Give me your favorite painting," he added impulsively. "It will be the perfect gift for Annabelle."

"Colt's fiancée?"

Nolan nodded. "She's quite the cook and she has twin daughters, Emily and Lucy."

Just as he'd hoped, Pepper's smile widened. He hadn't anticipated the punch of lust to his gut, though. What the hell?

This smoldering attraction was not welcome. Not. At. All. Memories were one thing, but layering in this fierce, unwanted need was simply not smart. Damn his libido.

"Sounds like Colt is a lucky man."

If a man wanted a family, sure. Colt and Annabelle were perfect together and had found solace in each other during a tough time. When Annabelle's father had literally gambled away their home to Colt, the two had sparred for a while before realizing they were crazy in love.

Love worked for some people, not for Nolan. Saving lives and being his own boss were more than rewarding as far as he was concerned. He'd tried the whole relationship thing with Pepper…and look where that had gotten him.

All he needed to do was continue on the way he had: dating, working, living day to day…ignoring that niggle of emptiness that crept up and choked him on occasion.

Nolan was more eager than ever to get to his date. He'd booked reservations at the classiest restaurant about an hour away and if things went as planned, he'd have no trouble taking her back to her place after. Because no woman ever went to his home. Ever. That was his sanctuary, a space he'd built on the back of Pebblebrook for privacy. That house held a special place in his heart and the reason why was standing right in front of him carrying another man's baby.

After glancing at his purchases spread out on the counter, Nolan pulled out his credit card. Once he had the items paid for, he slid the painting beneath his arm and grabbed the two vases. "Thanks, Pepper."

She folded her hands on the counter and nodded. "You're welcome. Be sure to tell your friends where to get gifts for their ladies."

"I definitely will." He swallowed hard, deciding to

go ahead and tell her what was weighing on his mind. "I'm sorry. I know I said that a long time ago, but…"

Her lids lowered for a second. Then she blew out a breath and met his gaze again. "It's over, Nolan. I'm focusing on my baby, this new life I'm rebuilding. I can't look back."

Rebuilding. How many times had she done that since he'd left her? Pepper had always been such a vibrant woman, always happy and smiling. The loss of their child had dimmed her spark, and the way he broke things off had doused what little flicker of light had remained. He'd often wondered over the years if she'd ever found joy again…or who she'd found it with.

More potential heartbreak was definitely something he couldn't and didn't want to deal with. The risk was too great to even entertain such thoughts.

They'd both done exactly what they'd set out to do. He was damn happy being a doctor and a rancher. And his bachelor status would remain intact. He was getting ready to help Colt gear up to open Pebblebrook as a dude ranch, so any spare time he had was taken.

"I wish you the best," he stated, the blasted guilt settling heavy in his chest. "See you around."

"Yeah, see you," she said softly.

With one final nod, Nolan headed out the door. He couldn't get out of Painted Pansies fast enough. Sleep deprivation could cause a man to start thinking about things, decisions he'd made and everything he'd given up to seek success.

But Nolan didn't have regrets on the path he'd taken. He did regret hurting Pepper, though, so much it cut him to the core. At one time he would've done anything for her, but in the end, they'd wanted different things and he couldn't be what she wanted.

Nothing had changed since then, either. He'd opted not to have a family after they lost their child. He wouldn't say he shut down exactly, but he'd certainly reevaluated what he desired in life and he knew for certain he wished never to go through that kind of anguish again.

Nolan carefully set the arrangements on the back floorboard of his SUV. This quaint shop Pepper had was perfect for her. For as long as he'd known her, she'd had a flare for art and creativity. She'd been a dreamer, one of the things he'd loved most about her.

Without looking back to see inside the wide storefront window, Nolan forced himself to move forward. Wasn't that what he'd always done? Pushed onward, no matter what was going on internally. That was what made him one of the best doctors around. He could compartmentalize his feelings and turn them off when needed.

The jumbled emotions he had after seeing Pepper were absolutely not something he was ready to face…no matter how attractive she still was. So he'd shut those feelings down, just like he had the last time he saw her.

Two

The aftermath of this date was quite the opposite of what Nolan had initially planned. But cutting the evening short had been his idea…and he was still second-guessing his decision.

He'd taken his date home and dropped her off with a lackluster kiss good-night. In hindsight, he could've put more enthusiasm into the kiss and should've been whisking her off her feet and to the nearest bed. Unfortunately, he hadn't been in the right frame of mind for a sexual romp or even dessert. He'd feigned not feeling well, when the reality was, he'd spent his entire night envisioning another woman.

Damn it. Pepper had barely stepped back into town and now he was totally off his game. Well, technically, she'd told him she'd been back a month, but he'd only seen her this morning. Bottom line…he'd not had any heads-up on her return. Clearly he'd been too busy working to familiarize himself with the latest gossip running amok in Stone River.

But deep down, he knew *nothing* could've mentally prepared him for how he'd feel when he saw Pepper after ten long years. Hell, he wasn't sure he could even put a name to it.

Nolan found himself heading toward Painted Pansies before he recognized what he was doing. Why was he even on this road? This was quite a bit out of the way of his home on Pebblebrook Ranch.

Thankfully, he was off tomorrow, because he knew he'd be up all night trying to figure out why in tarnation he was getting so—

What the hell?

Nolan saw the flames in the distance, but as he got closer, he realized they were shooting out the top-floor window of Pepper's building. They were small and only in the front, but nonetheless, fear gripped him like nothing he'd ever known.

In his line of work, Nolan was used to making life-and-death decisions under pressure. But this felt different, like a vise around his chest. With adrenaline pumping, he quickly dialed 911. Then he pulled off the road, rattled off the address, and raced from his SUV toward the back of Painted Pansies.

As he rounded the corner, he saw Pepper attempting to crawl out the window and onto the roof of the back porch.

"Pepper!" he shouted. "The fire department is on

the way. Climb onto the roof and I'll help you from there."

She threw a look over her shoulder, and Nolan's heart clenched. Pepper's face was filled with pure terror and she held one hand protectively over her abdomen. He couldn't think about that right now; he couldn't focus on the fact she'd lost one baby already and was most likely petrified as she tried to get out of this situation without causing harm to her unborn child.

All that mattered right now was getting her away from this fire. Nolan heard the approaching sirens and relief trickled through him.

"Come on," he urged. "You're almost to the roof."

Cautiously, she let go of the window ledge and crawled on her hands and knees over the roof until she reached the edge. She stared down at him as if she was afraid to jump.

"I'll catch you," he told her as he extended his arms. When she hesitated, he felt that adrenaline surge. "Pepper, come on."

"I can't fall," she cried.

"You won't," he assured her, knowing he'd never let her get hurt. "I promise."

And now was not the time to analyze the fact he'd hurt her immensely once before.

Sirens grew louder, but Nolan didn't take his eyes off her. She eased closer to the edge and gave him another look, and he nodded, silently pleading for her to trust him.

It seemed like slow motion, but Nolan knew the

time it took her to let go and fall into his arms was only a mere couple of seconds. He cradled her against his chest and ran back to his SUV. His pulse continued to pound fast, but not from carrying her. Pepper didn't weigh much; she'd always been petite. His work as a part-time rancher demanded he be physically fit, so even pregnant, she wasn't putting a strain on his muscles.

"I can walk," she told him breathlessly, but her arms encircled his neck as he crossed the street.

"And I can carry you. Did you get hurt? Inhale too much smoke?"

Pepper shook her head. "No. I was getting ready for bed when I smelled smoke and came out of the bathroom to see the front curtains in flames."

A chill coursed through his veins. What if she'd been asleep? What if she hadn't gotten out in time? What would she have done had he not been driving by? Would anyone have been around to help?

She trembled against him, and he instantly recognized the shock. The fire truck pulled up and in an instant the firefighters were working on the flames, which still seemed to be only in the front of the second story. An ambulance arrived right after, and Nolan swiftly carried her over.

"I'm Dr. Nolan Elliott." He addressed the two EMTs who came around to open the back of the ambulance. "I don't believe she was inside long, but I want her to have oxygen and be taken in immediately. I'll follow and get her admitted."

"I don't need to be admitted," she argued, but Nolan ignored her protest. She wasn't in charge here.

"She's pregnant," Nolan went on as he stepped up into the back, still holding her in his arms. He lowered her down onto the cot. "How far along?"

Her dark eyes met his and he had to ignore everything that had happened between them up until now. She was a patient. He had to compartmentalize.

"Pepper?"

"Seventeen weeks. Nolan, I don't think—"

"Oxygen," he said as one of the medics climbed in on the other side. "I'll meet you at the ER entrance."

Pepper gripped his arm as the oxygen mask was placed over her nose and mouth. She pulled it aside and shook her head.

"I don't need you there and I don't need to be admitted," she insisted. "I wasn't in the apartment that long. I'm not coughing and I'm not light-headed. I'm fine."

"And you're positive your baby is?" he retorted.

Her eyes narrowed but he didn't care if he angered her. In his years at Mercy, he'd seen it all and he wasn't taking a chance with Pepper and a baby...not again. Even though this wasn't his child, he wouldn't risk it.

Damn his desire to protect her.

"I'll go get checked out, only for the baby." Her hold tightened on his arm. "But you're not coming. I don't need you there."

Nolan stared at her another minute but didn't say a word. Finally, he met the gaze of the medic and nodded. No way was Nolan going to let her go alone. No matter what Pepper wanted, right now someone was going to look out for her and her child.

And it seemed he was the chosen one.

"This is ridiculous."

Pepper realized her argument was in vain. But as she sat in the passenger seat of Nolan's extremely flashy SUV heading up the drive to Pebblebrook, she also knew she had little choice but to go along with his plan.

Well, actually, he hadn't planned, more like *steam-rolled*. After he'd shown up at the hospital, despite her repeated requests that he stay away, he'd informed her he'd be taking her to his house to rest because it was nearly two in the morning and she couldn't go back to her apartment.

Her apartment. The one place she was going to try to set down roots, to build a life for her baby.

Yet here she was pregnant and temporarily homeless until she found out what damage had been done by the fire. Oh, and she was back with the one man who'd crushed her heart and her spirit and turned his back on her when she needed him most.

It went without saying that she'd had better days. Like the day she'd broken her arm in two places after she'd gone hiking and attempted to climb a vine over a ravine. Even then she was having a better time than she was now.

"I don't want to stay with you."

Nolan grunted and continued up the drive. Pebblebrook was exactly like she remembered. Magnificent, with rolling white fencing flanking the drive, the three-story main house was adorned with porches extending across the top two floors. The stables, which were nicer than most homes, brought back memories. Memories of spending evenings in the hayloft, riding horses over the acreage, sharing hopes and dreams.

They'd failed to discuss the one dream that had ultimately come between them, but that was water under the bridge. Pepper firmly believed everything happened for a reason… If only she could figure out why she was here now with Nolan.

"You tell me a logical place to drop you off in the middle of the night and I'll consider it."

Pepper crossed her arms and continued to stare out the window into the darkness. She really didn't care that she was acting like a child. After all, who could blame her? She was tired, scared, worried of what the future would hold for her as a single mother. Once again she'd gotten tangled up with a man who wanted nothing to do with a family or her. But at least this time she hadn't been in love.

Although she didn't need a man to complete her life or to help her raise the baby, she was sorry this child would never know his or her father. But Pepper was confident her child would be loved and cared for and would never feel the void.

"That's what I thought," Nolan muttered when she failed to answer him. "Now, you need to quit being stubborn and just relax for tonight."

"Stubborn? Relax?" Pepper whipped around in her

seat. "I'm not stubborn, you jerk. You pushed your way into the ER—"

"I actually flashed a smile at the charge nurse."

Rage boiled within her. "Just because you work there doesn't give you the right to steamroll me into agreeing to this."

"I didn't steamroll anybody," he said as he made a sharp curve in the drive. "I merely stated that you could be admitted or come home with me. Those were your two options whether you liked them or not. You have no other place to crash tonight."

Pepper scowled. As if she needed the reminder. She'd been racking her brain trying to work out what had happened in her apartment. She'd been burning some new melts she'd made that afternoon, but she was positive she'd turned off the warmer before she got into the shower. Hadn't she?

"I won't be your charity case so you can feel better about yourself over how you treated me in the past."

There. She'd laid it out there. Pepper didn't want there to be any question about where they stood. Because the truth was, she'd moved on. And the fact that the sight of Dr. Nolan Elliott made her weak in the knees and brought up so many unforgettable memories, both bad and good, didn't mean anything. She was a different woman now. And he was a different man.

But the way he wanted to come to her aid warmed something inside her...something she couldn't afford to let herself feel ever again.

"I'm not doing this out of some warped sense of

redemption, Pepper," he told her. "I have seven bedrooms and nine bathrooms. Stay here as long as you want until you make alternate arrangements. I won't even know you're there."

Yeah, but *she'd* know *he* was there. Did he truly believe she'd be comfortable on his turf? And why on earth had he built such a huge home when he was single? Had he married after she'd left? Pepper had purposely distanced herself from him and not doubled back to find out what Nolan had done with his life. She didn't want to know if he'd found another woman, created a life with her, had children. Because as hard as it was to admit, she feared that if he'd gone forward and had a family, she wouldn't have recovered from the crushing blow.

So, one night together was more than enough. Besides, she had more important things to contend with than licking old wounds. Like figuring out where to go if her apartment was a total loss. She only prayed the fire department was able to spare her shop because there was no plan B for income.

"I'm only staying tonight because I'm exhausted."

A two-story stone home came into view and Pepper's heart clenched with sorrow. Granted, it was dark, but the spotlights illuminated the incredible home enough to send her falling back into yet another memory.

This was the dream home they'd planned together. Everything from the stone facade to the thick wood columns leading up to the second-story porch. And if he'd stuck to the original plans, those doors on the top floor led straight to one impressive master suite, with a matching master suite at the other end of the hall.

He'd gone through with every plan they'd made… and he'd done so without her, as if she'd never had a place in his life at all.

Pepper covered her abdomen with her hands as Nolan pulled into an attached four-car garage. Of course each bay was filled with another impressive vehicle. A work truck, which looked fresh off the showroom floor, a sporty car and another SUV. Why did one man need this many cars and this large of a home?

Pepper wasn't a shrink, but she also wasn't naive. Clearly Nolan was trying to either compensate for something or fill a void in his life, and she was pretty sure he didn't need to overcompensate for anything.

And now, to add fuel to the fire, she was spending the night with the one man she didn't want to be attracted to, *shouldn't* be attracted to. But there was no denying Nolan was still just as sexy, just as powerfully commanding in that irresistible way that made her breath catch in her throat and her palms grow damp.

"You built our home." The words slipped out before she could stop them and now they hovered in the air between them.

"It's the only home I ever saw here," he replied.

Pepper turned in her seat. The garage lights lit up the interior of the SUV and she preferred when things were dark. From this angle she saw too much—and she worried what he'd see when he looked back at her.

She started to ask him more but decided none of his life was her business. He'd made that abundantly apparent, and she needed to remember that. Just because he'd rescued her from her burning building and hadn't left her side since, didn't mean he wanted to revisit their past. And she had too much on her plate to even think like this.

Clearly, she was exhausted.

"Pepper, I—"

"Just show me to my room." His blue eyes met hers, and Pepper held her breath. He still had the power to make her tremble without so much as a word. "I'm tired and need my rest. I have a big day tomorrow assessing damage and talking to the insurance and fire department."

He gave her a clipped nod. "I'll go with you."

"You're not going with me." Did he really think she needed someone to hold her hand?

She took in his dress shirt, his dark jeans, and realization slammed into her. Pepper closed her eyes and pulled in a breath. "Your date… I hope this didn't ruin anything."

"I'd already dropped her off when I was heading home."

For reasons Pepper didn't want to delve into, she was glad to know the recipient of the mixed bouquet went home alone.

"Well…if I didn't say it earlier, thanks."

Nolan stared at her another minute, his eyes dropping to her lips for a half second, but it was all she needed to know. He was affected by the fact they'd been thrust back together, albeit temporarily—it had made him leave his date.

Maybe coming back to Stone River hadn't been the best idea, but she was all out of options at the moment. All she had to do was get through this night and then she could make a concerted effort to dodge Nolan Elliott at all costs. Because she wasn't sure she could resist the temptation if she had to spend too much time with him.

Three

Despite how insistently Pepper protested, Nolan joined her the following morning at Painted Pansies to assess the damage. He used the excuse that he had to drive her, but he wouldn't have let her face this alone regardless.

The apartment wasn't a total loss, but she would not be living there anytime soon. Thankfully, the store wasn't harmed, but an electrician needed to come out to double-check things because the fire marshall was sure the spark that started the fire had come from the outlet her warmer was plugged into.

Nolan had already contacted someone and expected him shortly. Pepper wouldn't like that he'd taken over, but someone had to because she looked dead on her feet.

And, okay, maybe some of that past guilt was spurring his actions, but he knew that top-notch contractors could get things done quicker than she could if she were left to her own devices. There was no reason she should wait on insurance to get their act together, because they were notorious for being slow, and Nolan was just offering his aid. Money meant nothing to him and he could see that Pepper could use a break.

Pepper walked around the shop and into the back room. Nolan took in the window display with large canvas paintings and the flamboyant bouquets in various heights. Everywhere he looked, there was vibrancy, color, life. He knew Pepper had always envisioned something like this, but she'd been such a free spirit, wanting to travel the world, he'd never really thought she'd set down roots anywhere.

Of course, once upon a time, they'd planned on settling down together. They'd designed a house when they were so young and tossing one dream after another out into the wind, hoping they would catch.

Regret tightened the corners of his mouth. Some things just weren't meant to be, because when faced with reality, he hadn't been able to take charge. The death of their unborn baby made him too wary to consider going down that path again.

When someone tapped on the glass of the front door, Nolan jerked around. A middle-aged couple stood on the other side and he shook his head and pointed to the closed sign.

Behind him, Pepper let out a gasp.

Nolan glanced over his shoulder. "You know them?"

Her eyes remained fixed on the door as she nodded and pressed a hand protectively over her stomach. She'd thrown on one of his T-shirts and still had on the same shorts from last night. Her hair had been washed but left down to dry in long, silky ringlets. Desire pulsed through him. He knew exactly what that hair felt like between his fingertips and draped over his body, but now was not the time to get turned on. Still, his fingers itched to touch those luscious locks again, to see if they were just as smooth as he remembered.

"Want me to get rid of them?" he asked.

The tapping grew louder, more persistent.

"They've already seen me." Pepper raked a hand through her hair and finally looked his way. "I hate to ask this, but can you stay? I'm exhausted and this could get ugly. I know we're not necessarily friends or anything, but—"

"I'll stay."

Whoever these people were, Pepper wasn't happy about seeing them.

She crossed the store and placed one hand on the knob, the other on the lock. Throwing a look over her shoulder, she caught his eyes again. "Their son is the father of my baby. I've only met them once."

A sense of unease roiled through him. Of course, he knew nothing about the father of her baby, other than the fact he was obviously not in the picture at the moment, but his parents showing up here from…

wherever it was they were from was probably not good news for Pepper.

He bit back a curse. Why was he sticking around? Whatever Pepper had going on in her life was *her* concern, her business. He should be at Pebblebrook helping Colt with the ranch or coming up with things he could do at Hayes's house. Hayes was one of his other brothers, and he would be home from his deployment overseas in two weeks.

With four Elliott boys, there was always someone in need of a helping hand. Nolan hadn't seen Beau, Colt's twin, in nearly a year. He'd been too busy shooting one film after the next. That must be the life he loved out there in LA, because he rarely came home.

The flick of the lock pulled Nolan's attention back to the moment. Pepper moved back and opened the door.

The couple swept in like they owned the place. Nolan was instantly on alert. He didn't like to stereotype, but he figured he had these people pegged. Expensive clothes, flashy car on the curb… He knew how much that car was because he'd had one, as well, and sold it for an upgrade. The way the woman looked condescendingly down at Pepper had Nolan taking a step closer, his protective instincts kicking into high gear.

"Mr. and Mrs. Wright. What are you doing here?" Pepper asked.

"We didn't have a number to reach you, but Matt told us where you were moving to and we heard you opened a little shop in Stone River." Mrs. Wright glanced around the shop, her nose snarled as she turned back to Pepper. "Is this typically how you come to work?"

"I'm actually not open today." Pepper cast a worried look to Nolan. "We're doing some minor renovations."

The couple glanced to Nolan but immediately dismissed him. Most likely they figured him for the hired hand. That was fine. He wasn't here to make friends or to give a good impression. He was here for...what? To support Pepper, although she didn't want it and he had other things he really needed to be doing.

"Can we talk privately?" Mr. Wright asked quietly.

Pepper crossed her arms over her chest. "You can just tell me now."

"We have some...devastating news." Mrs. Wright swiped at her eyes, and Nolan knew that expression. He'd been a doctor long enough, had seen grief too many times to count. He took another step toward Pepper but resisted the urge to reach out and touch her. He wasn't sure what the Wrights were going to do and he didn't want to show his hand this soon and reveal that he and Pepper had a past. They didn't need to know.

"Matt had a heart attack two nights ago," the woman whispered as if speaking through the tears clogging her throat. "He didn't make it."

"Oh...no." Pepper reached a hand out for support and Nolan grabbed it right away, the worry for her far outweighing the need to keep his distance. "But he was so young," she murmured in disbelief.

Again, Nolan knew from experience that age meant nothing in the medical field.

"I know he told you he wanted nothing to do with this baby, but we do." Mr. Wright wasn't quite as emotional as his wife, and he seemed to be ready to get down to business. "We want full guardianship rights for the baby now that our son is…is gone.

"What?" she whispered, her eyes widening in shock.

"We're filing for sole custody. It just… It makes sense given how stable we are and the financial backing we can provide."

Pepper's hand tightened in Nolan's. "No, you can't do that. I don't even know you. Matt paid me. He gave me money to leave him alone and to invest however I wanted for the future of the baby, provided I never contact him again. He signed his rights away right before I left…"

Pepper seemed to be rambling out of fear, and Nolan knew in that second he'd do anything to keep this baby in her life. Forget what happened between them years ago. Pepper needed someone in her corner and he damn well wasn't going to leave her to face these vultures all alone. He owed her that much at least.

His chest constricted with guilt as realization struck. This Matt guy had treated Pepper like she was a burden…the same way Nolan had done years ago.

"Matt's gone now," the lady sniffed. "And we want

to raise our grandchild. We've already contacted our team of attorneys."

"What?" Pepper gasped.

"We aren't questioning your parental skills, but we feel the child would be better off with us," Mr. Wright reiterated. "We know our rights. We're determined to have a DNA test done to prove we're the grandparents. You have to be realistic here and see that we're more financially stable."

Nolan wrapped his arm around Pepper, which drew the attention of the other couple. "Pepper isn't going to discuss this any further without talking to her attorney. If you'll leave me your lawyers' information, I'll be sure to have someone contact them."

Because he had his own team on retainer and he would be calling them before the Wrights pulled away from the curb.

Mrs. Wright's eyes narrowed. "And who are you?"

There was no good way to answer that question and it was none of his concern anyway. "The contact information, please, and then you can go. Neither Pepper nor I will be discussing this any further without our attorneys present."

Beneath his touch, Pepper trembled. If she could hold it together long enough for him to usher them out the door, she could break down all she wanted later. Nolan just needed to get her alone.

Mr. Wright gave the name of a high-powered attorney in Houston. Nolan knew his team was better, more ruthless, and there was no way this couple would take Pepper's baby. Not as long as Nolan was in charge…and he had every intention of seeing this through.

Between the fire, the renovations and now this, Nolan didn't see himself pulling away from Pepper anytime soon. Which was fine in the grand scheme of things. He owed her more than he could ever repay. So somehow he'd just have to find a way to resist temptation and keep his hands to himself.

Nolan released Pepper long enough to open the door and gesture for the Wrights to leave. "Don't call or come back. Someone from my law firm will be in touch."

"Pepper, don't push us away," Mrs. Wright said over her shoulder. "You're carrying the only piece of our son that we have left."

Nolan closed the door and slid the lock back into place. Pepper continued to stare at the spot where the older couple had just stood. He gently gripped her arm and guided her toward the back room, where he eased her down onto an old wooden chair at the desk as he propped his hip along the edge.

"What am I going to do?" she muttered aloud as she continued to stare at nothing in particular. "I don't have an attorney and I can't compete with them anyway. Their money, their power. I can't let total strangers have custody of my baby."

She never once looked up at him as she rattled off her concerns. But Nolan was taking all of this in. He leaned down over the desk, bracing his weight on his hands.

"Look at me," he demanded. "I pay my lawyers

a hefty fee. They'll be on this case today and we'll make sure they don't take your child."

Pepper blinked, sending a tear spilling down her cheek. "I used all the money Matt gave me to invest into this place. I wanted a secure future."

A wave of fury surged through him. He hated this guy. Who the hell paid a woman to leave him alone?

Shame seized him once again. How had he been any different? He'd pushed her away with his actions, his harsh words. He'd been hurt from the loss of their baby—a baby he hadn't realized he'd wanted until it was gone.

"My team will take care of this. I'll put the call in now."

Pepper shook her head. "No. I'll handle this. I'm not leaning on you or anyone else."

While Nolan admired her determination, he wasn't about to argue with her idiotic logic. He shoved his hands in his pockets and rocked back on his heels.

"You have enough on your plate with this building and you said your funds were tied up here. How can you pay for an attorney? A good one you don't have to second-guess about whether he's doing what should be done to secure your child's future with you? How are you going to do that?"

Pepper's lips thinned as she shrugged one slender shoulder. "The same way I've gotten along these last ten years without you. I'll find a way."

He jerked in a breath. She was hurting, he understood that, but the jab she delivered had no doubt been bubbling below the surface just waiting to come out.

He deserved that, but he wasn't about to stick around for more verbal punches.

"My contractor is due here any minute to get an estimate ready for your insurance. I'll have my attorney call you today, too. Don't hold back with either guy and don't worry about the money."

"Says someone who's never worried about money," she muttered.

Nolan pulled his phone from his pocket. "I'm trying to help and then I'll stay out of your way. It's clear you don't want me around. I get that, Pepper, but I won't let you deal with all of this on your own."

Pepper tucked her hair behind her ears and nodded. "Fine. But I want an itemized list of all the charges so I can pay you back after the insurance kicks in. I may take a while, but I won't be indebted to you."

He wasn't getting into that now. But Nolan had no intention of taking a dime from her. She needed to be stress-free, to concentrate on this pregnancy and a healthy baby, not worry about her new business and a looming custody suit.

To keep the peace, he merely nodded and then headed toward the back to talk to his contractor. He wanted everything done right, sparing no expense. And a few upgrades wouldn't hurt in the apartment, either. Nolan wasn't certain what it looked like before, but he planned on personally seeing to it that it was all up-to-date, with state-of-the-art appliances, whatever it took to ensure Pepper had everything she needed to live comfortably.

It was the least he could do. And, yes, guilt spurred

his actions, but so what. He was a different man than he was ten years ago.

Except that part of him that still desired her. Damn it. After all this time of not seeing her, having her this close wasn't something he'd prepared for. She was sexy as hell, her figure a bit fuller from the pregnancy, but she was breathtaking. The fact she wore one of his T-shirts was even more arousing because he recalled many other occasions when she'd wear his shirt…only his shirt.

Nolan headed back to the ranch, determined to work out his frustrations on the farm. But first he needed to call his attorney. There was no way in hell those people were going to take Pepper's baby. Nolan would make certain of that.

Four

Pepper ended up opening her shop later in the day. There was no reason she couldn't work and she wanted to get her business up and running. She needed to be open to the public during peak hours, and thankfully, this old building was nestled right in the hustle and bustle of the small town.

Maybe if she spent some time on a painting to keep her mind occupied, that would help. Making something beautiful out of a blank canvas always calmed her nerves and right now she needed calm. Between the obvious stressful events of the fire and the contentious visit by the Wrights this morning, she was still reeling over the fact Nolan was so eager to offer help.

Throwing money around was the easy part, though. Perhaps that was the only way he could clear his conscience. Pepper didn't want his guilt to spawn his actions. If he wanted to help, she'd rather it be because he actually wanted to, not because he was trying to make amends for the past.

As Pepper set up her easel in the back room, the shop's phone rang. She glanced to the ID, but didn't recognize the number.

"Painted Pansies."

"Ms. Manning?" the deep male voice asked. "This is Jason Davis. I represent the Wright family."

Pepper gripped the edge of the table and slowly sank into the chair. Her heart clenched as fear squeezed it like a vise.

"Is there a time you and your attorney can meet with us?"

Pepper's mind raced. She hadn't even talked to an attorney, had no idea if Nolan had even called anyone yet. This was all so fast, so unexpected, she had no idea what to do.

"Mr. Davis, I'm not sure when we could meet." She hoped her voice sounded strong and confident, considering she was shaking like a leaf. "I'm speaking with my attorney today and he will be in touch."

She hoped.

"My clients are willing to offer you a generous amount—"

"I won't be bought or bullied, Mr. Davis. My lawyer will be in touch."

Pepper hung up, tossed the phone from her jittery hand and attempted to pull in a deep breath. She wasn't sure if she wanted to scream, cry or run away and never look back. Maybe all of the above?

No. She wasn't running. She'd left once before and had circled right back. She would stay and fight. This was where she'd put her roots down, where she'd raise her baby and grow her business. The decision had been made of necessity, but she'd chosen to stay because of her connections to this place.

Pepper had no idea who Nolan's attorney was or if he could even fight, but there was no way she was going to just hand over her child.

A pang of sadness swept through her. She did feel terrible that Matt was gone. He wasn't a bad guy. They'd been more friends than anything and he hadn't wanted to be a father, but she wasn't about to give his parents a replacement child. They might argue they had superior finances, but didn't that just prove they were more concerned about money than the actual welfare of their grandchild? Who would be heartless enough to want to rip a baby away from its mother?

Pepper shot off a text to Nolan asking about his attorney because she needed to speak with him ASAP. When the bell on her door chimed, Pepper sucked in a deep breath and forced herself to relax. She had customers she needed to tend to. Reputation was everything and she couldn't be in a bad mood with the public.

How simple would this all be if she could just lean on Nolan and use his power and influence to make the chaos and fear go away? She wanted her baby, her fresh start at life…and she wanted to seek solace in those captivating blue eyes of his.

Unfortunately, she couldn't turn to him, because they weren't over what had happened. They'd dodged the feelings, the hurt, the anger…and she'd left.

But she'd moved on. She'd grown up and she wouldn't give in to temptation no matter how kind and supportive he was being. She knew what it was like to get her heart broken by him.

Right now, though, she had to be a business-woman. She'd deal with Nolan later.

Oh, the irony.

Nolan still couldn't believe the conversation he'd had with his attorney, but the suggestion kept rolling through his head. At first he'd laughed, then he'd been appalled at the crazy notion, and now the idea had taken root and he could think of nothing else.

He had already spoken to his contractor and was told the renovations to the apartment could be done in two weeks. Pepper wouldn't like what he had to say, but Nolan wasn't backing down. She'd have to see that what he was about to present to her was her best option. Temporarily, of course.

Just as he pulled in front of Painted Pansies, Pepper turned her open sign off. She met his gaze through the large front window and stilled. Nolan knew she'd put up a fight, but this time, where she was concerned, he was holding his ground. He could do this and not lose himself in her. This was about making up for the past, not reigniting an old flame.

No more running…for either of them.

Those protective instincts had kicked in the moment he'd seen she was expecting and alone. Now with the fire and the custody case looming over her, Nolan had every intention of slaying every one of her dragons.

Remorse drove his thoughts, his actions. He refused to delve into all the reasons why he couldn't let her do this on her own.

As soon as he entered her shop, he flicked the lock on the door. Pepper stood behind the counter as if she wanted some barrier between them. Nonetheless, that wouldn't stop him from doing what he'd come to do.

And if he didn't broach this now, he'd talk himself out of it because this crazy idea embodied every fear, every doubt he'd ever had when it came to Pepper. Their crackling attraction aside, this was a risk he'd never thought he'd take again.

"I'm surprised you opened today," he told her.

She glanced down to her register and pulled out receipts. "I have to make money. The fire didn't do damage down here and I was able to salvage a couple of outfits that happened to be in my clothes dryer and were unscathed from the smoke and water."

He made a mental note to get her more clothes. Another thing she'd most likely balk at, but too bad. He wouldn't ask. If he had them purchased and delivered, she'd have no choice. Right?

"Did you have a productive day?"

Pepper blew out a sigh and finally stared up at him. "Did you stop by for small talk?"

Those piercing gray eyes were no less affective than they'd been a decade ago. She managed to touch him with just a look. And how she still had that power over him was beyond his comprehension.

Adjusting his hat, Nolan crossed the room and rested his arm on the top of the counter. "Not at all, Pepper, but I figured it was best to play nice because what I have to say may not put you in the best mood."

"I'm not in a good mood anyway, so why don't you just spit it out."

His eyes raked over the scoop neckline in her simple tank, his gaze heating at the sight of the thin cotton molding perfectly to her full breasts. She had on those bangle bracelets again and some long earrings in a variety of colorful stones. Her silky dark hair was still down from when she'd showered at his house, and all he could think of was how to get her back there again.

The image of her wet, naked, soapy in his oversize shower with the rain-head spray cascading down her gorgeous curves had him getting extremely hot and uncomfortable. Damn it, he still wanted her. There was no reason to even try to deny such a fact.

He had no right to her, but that wouldn't stop him. Pepper would be his again...at least temporarily. The ache he had for her had nothing to do with the past and everything to do with an all-consuming, burning need he hadn't expected upon seeing her again.

"You aren't seriously going to look at me like that," she stated, crossing her arms over her chest. "I can't be fooled by your charm."

"You're still just as beautiful," he drawled. "Makes a man want to admire the view."

Pepper shook her head and focused back on her receipts. "I'm immune to you now, so just say what you have to say and go."

Adorable that she thought things were that neat and tidy between them. They'd never been so structured. Back in the day, they'd been wild and young and free. Then life had thrown hurdles in their path and they hadn't survived the fallout. Now they were back to square one and nothing about this situation was simple.

"You never answered my text," she said tersely as she sorted the slips of paper. "If you don't want to help, that's fine. But if you could pass along the name of a good attorney, I'd appreciate it. The Wrights' lawyer called me and I had no idea what to say—"

Nolan was around the counter and taking her shaky hands in his as she rambled on. "Breathe," he commanded. "Just calm down and tell me exactly what their lawyer said."

Pepper removed her hands from his and flattened them over the papers. She dropped her head between her shoulders. "Just give me the name. I don't want you involved."

Too late for that, he thought ruefully. If she didn't want him interfering now, she'd be really ticked when he dropped the ultimate bomb. He'd gone further than just reaching out to his law firm.

"I already spoke with my attorney earlier—he's

on it. I was at the ranch helping Colt, so I didn't get to text you back, but I have this all under control."

With her hair curtained around her face, Nolan couldn't make out her expression, but he knew she was exhausted. Most likely she also felt defeated and/or cornered.

"Pepper, I'm only looking out for you and you're going to have to let me. I'm not trying to make this more difficult."

"Can you look at this from my perspective?" she asked as she slowly turned toward him. "Can you imagine finally having your entire life planned out only to have it crash down all around you, then have to come face-to-face with your past and pretend nothing happened?"

Nolan grabbed her shoulders, hauling her against his chest. Pepper's head tipped back as she stared up at him with wide, tormented eyes.

"You think this is easy? Seeing you again, knowing you're carrying another man's child?"

Nolan hated that he wasn't more in control, but there was no way he could lie to her, to himself. The fact she was pregnant again gutted him and reminded him exactly what he'd given up.

"I'm going to help you through this and you're damn well going to put the past aside and let me."

"Put the past aside?" she jerked out of his hold and took a step back. "It's not that simple, Nolan."

He rubbed his hand over the back of his neck. "I didn't mean it like that," he corrected. "I know we have unresolved issues and there is so much that needs to be put to rest, but for now, we need to work on your current situation. I need you to hear me out."

Pepper rested one hand on the counter and propped the other on her hip. "Fine. What's your miraculous plan?"

They'd reached the part of the conversation he'd rehearsed over and over again, but he had a feeling no matter how he delivered this, she would refuse. He expected, and deserved, no less.

"My contractor said your apartment would be ready in two weeks." There—laying some ground-work for his defense was probably best. "You can stay with me until then."

When she opened her mouth to argue, because she would without a doubt have a snappy comeback, Nolan held up a hand. "You have nowhere else to go and my house is plenty big enough. Besides, I'm on call and at the hospital so much you won't even see me most of the time."

That seemed to pacify her as she shut her mouth and nodded.

"What about the attorney? Does he think he can help? Because I can't lose this baby, too."

Too. That simple word said so much, yet left even more hurtful, accusing words hovering in the air between them. They would have to face that dark time in their lives eventually. Yes, they were two totally different people now, but he'd destroyed her and he would somehow, someway, make this right. Then he could move on once and for all—guilt-free.

But first things first. For now, Pepper and her child were his top priority.

"You're not losing the baby and I'm doing everything I can to make this less stressful for you," he informed her.

"Their attorney wants to meet with me and my lawyer."

She bit her lip as her chin quivered. That sight alone was like a punch to Nolan's gut. What kind of people came after a pregnant woman? Granted, this was their grandchild and their son had just passed away, so they were understandably grieving, but there was a better way to approach seeing the baby. If they wanted to fight dirty, Nolan would spare no expense because he wasn't about to let Pepper carry this burden all on her own.

"We will all go meet with them," he said.

His heart kicked up because there was no more dodging the rest of this. Not only did he worry how she'd take this, but he would be lying if he didn't admit he was hesitant because of his own sanity. Could he really go through with this?

Pepper stared back at him with those wide, expressive eyes. This was the same woman he'd fallen in love with as a teen, the woman he'd thought he'd spend his life with, the woman who had carried his child.

Their bond ran deep, but even if that didn't exist, he would find her sexy as hell. Her fiercely independent attitude was just an added layer to the enticing allure of this new Pepper Manning. Damn if he didn't admire her for moving on and doing exactly what she wanted.

But he'd caught her looking at him. Raking her eyes over him as if she was struggling with that same internal battle.

Yeah, they had quite a bit left to hash out between them and throwing this bomb onto that already-smoldering fire was only going to further complicate matters.

"You're not going with me," she told him with a stubborn lift of her chin. "I'm still not so sure about this whole idea of moving in with you for two weeks. There has to be somewhere else I can stay."

Nolan closed the space between them. "You'll be staying with me because we're getting married."

Five

"Married?"

She couldn't have heard him correctly. Because there was no way in hell she'd marry anyone right now, especially Nolan.

"My attorney said if you were married, that would be another bonus for our side."

Our side?

He explained this as if they were discussing a side order at a fast-food restaurant. How could he be so calm? This wasn't some joke or a test-drive on a car. This was real life—*her life*. There was a baby involved and Pepper refused to bring a child into such an unsteady world.

"I'm not marrying you." She turned back to her receipts, not that she could think about her sales right now, but she needed something to do with her hands. "And if that's the only way your lawyer thinks we can win, then I'll seek my own legal representation."

Nolan's hand covered hers. The strength, the warmth, that familiar touch had Pepper closing her eyes. These pregnancy hormones were already out of control, and adding a dose of this potent man was not helping.

Those devastatingly attractive good looks aside, he seemed hell-bent on helping her. How could she let him get close to her again? She didn't trust him. But more than that, her body still responded when he was around and getting in deeper with him now was a chance she didn't think she could take.

Was he aiding only out of guilt?

Honestly, at this point, she'd take his guilt and help if it meant holding on to custody of her baby. Money was one thing, but…marriage?

"Listen to me." Nolan's low, matter-of-fact tone demanded she hear him out. "I know the irony of this is hurtful, but if we show we're married, that we are making a life for this baby, it will look better in court."

Pepper stared at his large hand on top of hers. "I don't want to go to court. I don't want to be in this position at all." She tilted her head to glance at him out of the corner of her eye. "I want to get my business growing, have my baby and be left alone."

Beneath that black hat, Nolan's sharp blue eyes held her in place. "Sounds like a lonely life."

"Maybe being lonely is what I'm after," she countered with more bite to her tone than she'd intended.

She pulled in a deep breath, instantly filling her nostrils with his masculine, woodsy cologne or aftershave or just plain Nolan. He didn't smell like he'd worked on a ranch most of the day. He smelled *amazing* and Pepper was having a difficult time concentrating. Her traitorous heart beat wildly in her chest. He stood so close, smelled too tempting, and that touch was all too familiar.

Pepper sighed. She wanted to be angry with Nolan for the rest of her life, but she had grown since she'd left. If she gave in to this physical attraction now, she'd be going backward. She'd come so far during their time apart, but she was having trouble differentiating what she should do from what she wanted to do.

"The Wrights are going to come after you with everything," he added. "There's no way to sugarcoat this. They're going to look at your background, your work ethic, your finances, your boyfriends... Everything in your life will be used against you. Let's cut them off before they gain any momentum and perhaps they'll back off."

Pepper eased around, her swollen belly brushing against his taut abs. "Why are you doing this? What's in it for you?"

Nolan stared back at her, completely void of emotion. She wanted to know his angle, to understand what he was thinking, but as always, he was holding everything inside.

With no more energy for a verbal battle, Pepper

gathered her receipts together and shoved them all into her bank bag. She'd look at them later.

"I'm not marrying you."

As she started to move around him, he grabbed her elbow. That firm grip sent a burst of arousal rushing through her. One touch, that was all it took. How did he do that?

Pepper refused to meet his gaze. Having him this close and constantly touching her that way was too much to deal with on top of everything else.

"Don't do this," she whispered.

"I'm not giving up, Pepper. You need me, whether you want to admit it or not. The marriage would be temporary, long enough to untangle you from this mess. We'll get an annulment after."

Meaning they wouldn't consummate their marriage. Wow, this proposal just got more and more romantic. Her heart was all aflutter.

"I won't be married to a man who has girlfriends on the side to appease him."

Nolan's eyes dropped to her lips. "I'm more than happy to let you appease me, but that would put a damper on our annulment."

Pepper didn't want her body to tremble at the picture he painted. She knew all too well what an amazing lover Nolan was. And he was trying to wear her down. If she wasn't careful, he'd succeed.

"We're not getting married, so *that* puts a damper on this annulment."

She slid from his grasp and headed into the back room. She'd never gotten around to that painting she wanted to start earlier. Her blank canvas stared at her, just waiting for her to transform it. She could really use the stress reliever, but right now she didn't have the time or the energy.

All day she'd wondered where she would stay tonight. She could technically sleep in her bedroom upstairs. The damage was mostly contained to the living room and kitchen. But it still smelled like smoke and she shouldn't be inhaling that.

"You know this is the only way."

Pepper cringed as Nolan followed her. "I'm sure I can think of something."

There *had* to be a plan B. She refused to believe otherwise. What kind of example would she set for her child if she perpetually depended on someone else to help her out of a bind?

"Is that so?"

His smug tone had her stilling, but she kept her back to him.

"Because if you marry me, you'll have that much more leverage over them. We have a past, so nobody will think it's a lie. You have nowhere to go, Pepper, and you know firsthand that my home is more than large enough. You never have to see me."

But she wanted to. Even after all this time, with all that remained between them, she wanted to see him. She had that damn flutter whenever he was around. He captivated her on a deeper scale than before, despite all the alarm bells clamoring in her head.

"As I mentioned before, I'm at the hospital most

days," he went on. "Come home with me and we'll sort it all out."

Pepper pinched the bridge of her nose as resignation sank in. She was out of options and knew it was pointless to keep fighting the inevitable. "I'll come home with you—for now—but no more talk of marriage."

She turned to face him, realizing he was so much closer than she'd thought, she lost her balance as she tried to step back. He reached out to steady her, clasping her arm with one hand and molding his other hand over her rounded belly. That instinct to protect her and her child warmed the area in her heart he'd left so cold, so broken.

How did she resist these feelings when he kept trying to infiltrate her defenses?

"I'll drive you," he rasped, still holding on to her. "First we're going to stop and buy you some clothes and whatever else you need."

"I don't need clothes. I have a few things upstairs—just let me grab them."

Nolan shook his head and drew his hands away. "They smell like smoke. This is nonnegotiable."

Pepper glared at him. "I'm not about to be bullied into anything, not by you and not by the Wrights."

The edge of Nolan's mouth quirked into a half grin. Damn if that wasn't sexy with the combination of those cobalt eyes and dark lashes.

"Good," he replied smoothly. "I'd hate to think you were letting people walk all over you."

Pepper couldn't help but roll her eyes. "Oh, please.

Like you don't love this power trip you're getting by backing me into a corner. I'm not the same girl you hurt, Nolan. Nothing will happen between us ever again, no matter if I'm under your roof or not."

That smirk turned into a full-fledged smile. Damn him. Something inside her shifted—maybe it was pregnancy hormones or maybe she'd just gone mad. Regardless, Pepper was going to take full advantage of this opportunity. She'd lost so much, too much, and if Nolan was determined to help, then she'd take it. On her terms…which meant she may have to ignore her fears and give in to this preposterous marriage plan.

"But I'm willing to discuss some arrangements," she added, playing this out through her mind as the plan molded together. "You're paying the contractor for the renovations, which we agreed on, but I also know you're going overboard and not just putting things back the way they were."

Nolan merely nodded and remained quiet…still with that smug grin and mesmerizing gaze boring into her beneath his Stetson.

"And I'm sure you have your attorney pushing everything aside to help me with this case, which I appreciate." Guilt was a powerful tool. Pepper didn't like to play games, but if he thought this would somehow vindicate his actions, then she'd let him. "I'll live in your house. I'll marry you in name only. We won't sleep in the same room. We won't consummate the marriage."

The muscles in his jaw tensed and his lips thinned, but he finally said, "Fine."

"And you'll not be buying flowers for any more cute little nurses or any other woman. This marriage may be temporary and for pretenses only, but I won't have you unfaithful. The last thing I'd need is for word to get out that you're cheating on me."

He never took his eyes off her. Pepper wasn't sure what he was thinking, but if he truly wanted to help her, this was how he could do it.

"I already proposed something similar," he stated as he took a half step forward until he came toe-to-toe with her. "But I'm not sure you'll be able to stay with me and hold up your end of the deal with not consummating the marriage."

When he leaned closer to her ear, Pepper's breath seized in her chest.

"You remember exactly how it used to be," he whispered roughly. "And you'll start to wonder what we'd be like together now. Are you sure you can be in the bed so close to mine and not slip down the hall in the middle of the night?"

Pepper shut her eyes, imagining just that. It would be so easy to give in to this attraction, because she couldn't deny that physically she wanted him. Those weren't old feelings, either. Nolan Elliott was one sexy doctor, cowboy, knight to the rescue…even though his armor was tarnished.

Regardless, she *would* have this marriage annulled. Therefore, they had to keep their clothes on and their hands off each other. There was too much at stake to let sex screw things up. The entire situation was going to take a giant leap of faith on her part because if she didn't keep her heart guarded, she feared how she would be at the end of this farce of a marriage.

Pulling in every ounce of strength and courage she possessed, Pepper backed up until she bumped into the table her easel sat on. Straightening her shoulders, she stared directly at him, refusing to be intimidated by that intense blue gaze.

"The marriage will be quiet, at the courthouse and only temporary. As soon as this case is cleared up, you and I will get this annulled just as quietly. I'm only agreeing to this because my baby comes first and I need my life to be secure before I bring her home."

"Her?"

Pepper shrugged. "I actually have an appointment with a new obstetrician next week and I'll be finding out the sex. Don't get distracted. This baby is not your concern—you made it clear a long time ago that you didn't want that family life."

"As long as you're in my house and married to me, you're both equally my concern."

Pepper hated that she was accepting his charity, because that was what it boiled down to. But she had to be realistic. She'd used all of her funds from Matt to open Painted Pansies. Thankfully the building had already been in her family. Still, she'd had to pay for new flooring, lighting and decor, and all the start-up costs that went into a brand-new business.

Acceding to the inevitable, Pepper smoothed her hair behind her ears and stared up at Nolan. "So, when are we getting married?"

Six

"You may now kiss your bride."

Nolan rested his hand on Pepper's side as he leaned in, but she turned her head just enough so that his lips brushed against the corner of her mouth.

So that's how this would be. She was sticking to her guns and freezing him out. Fine. He could wear her down. Because she was his wife and he fully intended to get her into his bed before all was said and done.

In a swift move, he framed her face and tilted it to capture her lips. He'd be damned if he started this marriage without kissing his bride.

He didn't care if this sham of a union ended in a divorce or an annulment. The final result would be the same and that was all that mattered to him. His biggest struggle now was the fact he burned with desire for his wife.

He wasn't looking for a ready-made family, but he wanted Pepper. No matter what had happened in the past, no matter that she was expecting another man's baby, his attraction for her hadn't diminished. If anything, the fierce need he had for her was stronger than ever.

Today she wore her hair down with soft curls on the ends. Her short, simple white dress had flowy sleeves and fit over her abdomen to show off her gently rounded belly. She had on her bangles again and a pair of fat gold hoops. The little gold sandals on her feet were just as simple as everything else.

Yet Pepper took his breath away. He didn't want this pull any more than he wanted this marriage. But he owed it to her to help her out of this mess that she had become ensnared in. Having her in his home would be trying because he never brought women to his house. That was his sanctuary, his safe haven from the stresses of the outside world. He was putting literally everything on the line for her.

Pebblebrook was his life when he wasn't at the hospital and that was a part of himself he wasn't willing to share. His career, his need to serve others and make a difference, overrode anything else.

Once their child died, something in him had switched gears and turned him completely away from any type of commitment. That was a level of heartache he simply couldn't experience ever again.

He was the oldest of the Elliott boys and there was

a self-imposed expectation to do great things. While he loved the ranch, he'd always wanted to achieve more. But it wasn't always that way. There was a time he'd wanted a family, but once Pepper left, he'd started focusing on his career goals, throwing himself into the next chapter of his life so he didn't have to revisit the past.

His father had told him he worked too hard and wasn't enjoying life. He had enjoyed it with Pepper, but fate had had other plans for both of them.

Nolan extended his elbow to escort Pepper from the old office building at the courthouse. Not the most romantic setting, but then again, romance had no place here.

"Now what?" she asked as they stepped out into the thick Texas heat. "Do you need to call your attorney?"

He assisted her down the concrete steps toward his SUV parked out front. "I notified him last night. But he needs more information from you and we will have to meet with the Wrights and their lawyer."

Nolan opened her car door, but she turned to him instead of getting in. "Thank you. That sounds ridiculous, but you're going out of your way for me and my baby. I know this is some way for you to make amends for the past, and honestly, nothing can change that, but I need this plan to work. I can't lose my child."

Every primal instinct in him wanted to protect her, to shield her from everything trying to drag her down.

Unfortunately, she wasn't his. This brief marriage

would end as soon as he felt she was safe—and he'd spare no expense when it came to legal fees. He'd fight for her because she deserved this second chance at fulfilling her dream of having a family.

"You won't lose this baby," he assured her, taking her hands in his. "I have a hectic work schedule over the next few days, but I'll set up a time with my lawyer when we can both meet with him."

Once they were on their way back to the ranch, the irony of their circumstances fully hit him. He was bringing his pregnant wife back to a ranch house they'd designed years ago. Only this wasn't his baby, this wasn't his forever bride, and there would be no honeymoon phase.

"You don't have to check in with me." Pepper finally broke the silence as he pulled into the drive. "I don't have to know your every move."

Keeping that wall of defense firmly in place was her coping mechanism. She couldn't let this get too personal, or any more personal than it already was. Her heart had to come out of this unscathed.

"I know this isn't how you planned your life going once you came back," he told her.

He waved to Colt as he passed the stable. There would definitely be some explaining to do, but he'd get to that later. He'd been so preoccupied with helping Pepper he hadn't even told his brother she was back in town, let alone that he'd married her.

When Nolan had taken Annabelle her flowers and painting for her birthday, Colt hadn't been home. Nolan was guaranteed to take some flack for this, especially since Nolan had given some to Colt when he'd been messing with Annabelle by blackmailing her into getting the adjoining property.

It wasn't that long ago that Annabelle was Colt's neighbor and fighting to keep her land. Then nature took its course and Colt ended up falling in love with not just Annabelle, but her precious twin girls, too. Now their properties were legally joined.

Pebblebrook was now in the third generation of ranching, but Colt was the backbone behind the operation. Their father had long dreamed of expanding and opening a dude ranch, but he now suffered from dementia and was living in a nursing facility. Nolan visited as often as he could, sometimes even in the middle of the night after his shifts. He'd stop in and sit by his father's bed and, in the peaceful quiet, remember the man he used to be.

What would he think of Nolan marrying Pepper under these circumstances? When everything fell apart ten years ago, his father had been disappointed that Nolan had let Pepper go.

He'd made a mistake, one he could never rectify, but he was starting fresh now. And once this marriage was over, they'd go their separate ways and he'd be guilt-free. In theory that sounded amazing, but he didn't think things would go quite that smooth.

"I was hoping to avoid you completely," she replied, jarring him from his thoughts.

Nolan glanced toward her, noticed her staring down at the pewter-and-diamond ring he'd slipped on her finger moments ago.

That ring had been his mother's. Since Nolan was the oldest, he'd gotten it when she'd passed. With the last-minute marriage, he'd opted to get this out of his safe and give it to his temporary wife.

Pepper didn't have to know where the ring came from, because she would read too much into it. She didn't have to know that years ago he'd planned the perfect proposal with that very ring, but the pregnancy happened, then the miscarriage, and he'd withdrawn from getting too close and opted to throw himself into his career.

He hadn't been there for her when she'd been grieving and she'd left Stone River before they could settle things. It was still for the best that she'd gone, though. After the miscarriage, they weren't the same couple they'd once been, and they sure as hell weren't the same now that they'd been apart.

"You can still avoid me," he told her as he maneuvered into his four-car attached garage. "Take the bedroom on the opposite end of the hall. It's another master suite and nearly identical to mine. That's where I had all your clothes delivered anyway."

He'd been tempted to have them put in his closet, but there was no reason to make this more difficult for Pepper. Besides, he came and went all hours of the night and he wanted her to be able to feel free to move about his house. Having her here wasn't easy, though. She infiltrated his space, putting his heart at risk once again. The pull was tough to fight because he couldn't even pretend he didn't want her.

But he had to attempt to keep some control over his emotions.

"I have a pool, so feel free to take advantage of that anytime."

Pepper laughed. "You're going to make it hard to go back to my apartment when all this is done."

Nolan grimaced.

"Wow, you still have that same look." She gripped her door handle and jerked it open. "Don't worry. I'll still leave when this case is over and you can go back to the life you chose."

Like hell. Did she think he'd be untouched by this whole marriage? Did she honestly believe he'd just go back to his old ways now that she'd reentered his life?

Before she could exit, Nolan grabbed her arm and leaned over the console so his face was within a breath of hers. "You have no idea the life I want. You know the man I used to be, so stop telling me what you think you know."

Her eyes widened as her tongue darted out to swipe across her bottom lip. Nolan was barely hanging on and she wasn't helping. She had no clue the power she still held over him...he hadn't realized it himself until he'd seen her vulnerable and alone and being verbally attacked.

She still did something to him, something deeper than just physical attraction. Maybe it was that protective instinct overriding common sense, because he shouldn't want to keep touching her, but he couldn't stop himself. Hell, he didn't *try* to stop himself.

"I didn't get to properly kiss my bride at the ceremony. I want privacy this time."

Pepper's eyes widened a second before he captured her mouth beneath his. He cursed himself for being such a fool, as if passion and desire could erase years of hurt and emptiness.

But she tasted so sweet and when she opened for him that Nolan was lost. Again, that power she had no inkling she held was dragging him under. Relinquishing control had never been an option, but right now he had no choice. Pepper was drawing him in deeper and deeper. They'd been married for thirty minutes...there was no way they'd make it weeks, or even months, without tearing each other's clothes off.

Nolan drew back but slid his hand up to gently cup the side of her face. Pepper's lids slowly opened, feverish desire staring back at him. But she blinked a few times, as if pulling herself back from the moment.

"Don't do that again," she whispered.

"No?" His thumb stroked along that lush bottom lip. "Because it sure felt like you wanted me to not only do it again but take you inside and finish it."

Pepper whipped away from him and rushed out of the car, slamming the door on anything else he was about to say.

He winced. Well, that had gone about as well as he'd expected. He actually hadn't even planned on kissing her.

Okay, that was a lie. He had planned on kissing her, often actually. Why did he have to keep fighting this desire? Maybe he should take her to his bed, convince her to finally give in to what they both wanted. She wasn't immune to this sexually charged energy between them, but she was resisting it with everything she had. Maybe a little seduction was exactly what they both needed. And maybe he wanted to see if things were just as good as he remembered.

But wooing her into his bed would take careful planning and finesse. After all, that kiss had completely backfired on him and it was apparent he needed to up his game. He had to prove to her that their attraction couldn't go ignored…the question was, how?

Nolan raked a hand over the back of his neck and figured he might as well go talk to Colt and let Pepper cool off…or think about that kiss, because he sure as hell would.

Pepper stared around her bedroom and tried to calm her breathing. Even taking in the beauty of the room with the four-poster king-size bed, the sheers surrounding it and the double doors leading onto the balcony did nothing to settle her. She'd appreciate the aesthetics later.

She wasn't sure what she needed to get control of more—her anger or her desire.

How dare he just kiss her like he had the right? Like she wanted him to?

No. Nolan Elliott did whatever the hell he wanted, just like he always had. Did he honestly believe that now that they were married, she'd be in his bed? Not likely. Arrogant jerk.

Pepper slammed the door to her bedroom. Childish to go around slamming doors, but she wasn't quite sure what to do with all her emotions right now. She truly feared if she started crying, she might never stop. If she thought it would help, she'd throw something, but then she'd just be even more indebted to him than she already was. Besides, she wouldn't give him the satisfaction of knowing he had such a powerful hold over her.

Life was so much simpler when she traveled from place to place, taking odd jobs and then moving on to another city. No ties, nothing to break her heart all over again.

Yet she'd circled right back around and landed on Nolan's doorstep…literally.

Pepper crossed the spacious room and headed toward the double docrs of the most impressive walk-in closet she'd ever seen. Complete with an island in the middle, this spacious room was every woman's fantasy. The island was full of shoes tucked in each divider. Along the top was jewelry all laid out on display. Hanging in her closet was a variety of clothing, still with the tags dangling.

Slowly, she took a step forward. She trailed her fingertip over the simple jewelry. Colorfully beaded bangles, long, simple gold chains with delicate charms, oversize earrings. It was like the man knew exactly what she'd pick out. And he did. He knew her better than anyone because he'd been the only person she'd ever let that intricately into her life.

Even though all those years had separated them,

Nolan was so in tune with her…and that was what scared her the most.

Pepper turned toward the clothing and started pushing hanger after hanger aside, each piece made for her growing belly. Neatly stacked in the shelves along the wall were pajamas, bras, panties.

Part of her wanted to relish in this moment. The other part wanted to tell him her forgiveness couldn't be bought.

But the biggest part of her was still stuck on that kiss.

She'd be lying if she said she hadn't enjoyed it. Nolan had always known how to kiss to make her feel alive, to make her want so much more than just his mouth on hers. Being held by him again, kissed by him again, only proved her emotions had never died. No, they'd just been lying stagnant for years and were now flooding to the surface.

Pepper spun in a slow circle, still amazed at how Nolan had managed to pull all this off in such a short amount of time. No doubt he paid someone a hefty sum and when he snapped his fingers, his employee immediately complied.

She sank onto the cushioned bench across from the floor-to-ceiling mirror. How had her life landed her right back where she swore she'd never come?

When she met Matt in Houston at a party of a mutual friend, they'd immediately hit it off. The attraction had been there, but they didn't have the same life goals.

They'd enjoyed each other's company, both in bed

and out, and when she got pregnant, she'd known he wasn't going to get down on one knee or anything, but she really hadn't expected him to be so cold about it, either. The way he threw money at her to extricate him from the situation had stunned her at first, but she didn't want anyone in her baby's life who didn't want to be there.

The fear of this custody issue was becoming more and more real. Pepper spun the ring on her finger, glancing down to the sparkling stone. Ten years ago she would've given anything to have Nolan place a ring on her finger. She would've supported him in his journey to become a doctor, to be a part-time rancher, to save the world because that was what he'd been destined to do.

But he couldn't save their relationship. He hadn't even tried, yet he was bending over backward to save her now.

Did he have regrets? Of course he felt remorse for the obvious hurt he'd caused, but did he lament letting her go? Had he thought of her over the years and wondered how their lives would've been had she not miscarried? Would he have eventually come around and seen that a baby wasn't the end of life as they knew it and he could still have it all?

Or what if he'd stuck by her side through the pain and anguish of losing a child? Would they have grown stronger and maybe gone on to have more children?

Pepper cursed herself for getting caught up in that nostalgic what-if game. Sliding a hand over her belly, she smiled when she felt the slight shift beneath her palm. She actually loved being pregnant. Pepper relished each and every moment, knowing how fortunate she was to get a second chance at motherhood, and had even welcomed the morning sickness. She hadn't had that the first time.

The mere thought of Matt's parents taking her child away brought on a whole new level of fear. Surely no judge would award custody to them. Their money and their attorney were her biggest barrier, however. Pepper knew she was no match for that.

So she'd play the dutiful role of Mrs. Elliott if that meant she'd keep her child. She'd sell her soul to the devil himself if that ensured her a life without worry that her baby would be ripped from her arms.

Pepper came to her feet, staring at all the brand-new items just for her. She might not have sold her soul to the devil, but she wasn't too far off the mark. Knowing Nolan, she had no doubt he'd go out of his way to make sure she was comfortable, without a worry, and he'd take on everything to make her feel secure.

Between the sweet gesture and the touching and kissing, he was proving to be a perfect husband. Damn it. She didn't want this marriage to feel real or right or anything else, for that matter. She wanted to count down the days until they were done, but right now she didn't even want to think of the end.

In other words, Nolan was going to make it extremely difficult not to fall in love with him all over again.

Seven

Nolan had barely stepped foot in the stables when Colt came out of one of the stalls muttering beneath his breath.

It was late and all the workers had already gone home, but Colt was happiest right here with the horses. Well, that was where he used to be the happiest. Now he was pretty cozy with his fiancée, Annabelle, and her twin girls. They made the picture-perfect family.

Nolan's boot scuffed against the stone walkway between the stalls, and Colt jerked his head up. With a flick of his finger, he tipped his hat.

"Hey, man. Not out saving lives this evening?"

Nolan shook his head. "Too busy getting married."

Colt started to reach for the door on the stall and froze. "Excuse me?"

"I got married today."

Colt's eyes went to Nolan's hand, but he held up his ringless finger. "I don't have a band. I probably should get one."

He'd been so worried about Pepper having one that he'd not even thought of getting a wedding band for himself.

"What the hell are you talking about?" Colt exploded.

The reality of the day settled in and Nolan crossed to one of the benches on the wall between the stalls. He sank down and rested his elbows on his knees, suddenly feeling the weight of the world on his shoulders as he glanced down wearily at his boots.

The constriction in his chest seemed to tighten even more, like a vise grip around his heart. He'd pushed Pepper away so long ago, had been so harsh and cold to her because of his own uncertainties and fear. Yet here he was married to her and she was up at his home right now awaiting his return.

Everything had happened so fast in the past couple of days he wasn't even sure he believed he was actually married.

"Pepper is back in town," he mumbled, as if that blanket statement explained everything. "She's in a bind, so we got married."

Nolan glanced up to see the reaction on his youngest brother's face. Colt merely leaned against the stall door on the opposite side of the walkway and gestured for him to continue.

"Care to fill in the giant gap in between her coming to town and you saying 'I do'?"

Blowing out a breath, Nolan eased back on the bench. "She opened a new shop in town. That's actually where I got Annabelle's present for her birthday. I went in and had no clue it was Pepper's store. She's pregnant."

"Oh, hell," Colt muttered. "Are you all right?"

Nolan nodded. Did he have a choice?

"She was living in the apartment over her store," he stated. "It caught fire the other night. I've got Wayne working on it now, but then the grandparents of the baby came to confront her when she was already down. Their son had a heart attack and passed away."

"Damn. I take it Pepper and the guy weren't together anymore?"

Shaking his head, Nolan added, "He paid her a lump sum for support and asked to be left out of the upbringing."

The silence that followed that tidbit was a bit uncomfortable.

"Now his parents want custody," he went on. "They're a pretty powerful family."

"We're more powerful."

Nolan met his brother's determined gaze. "We are," he agreed. "My attorney joked that if she were married, there would be even more leverage for her case. So—"

"You jumped in to play white knight to make up for past sins."

Colt's tone wasn't accusing, more understanding, and Nolan was thankful he didn't have to explain. Apparently love had softened Colt, because a few months ago his brother would have been tearing him up for getting involved with Pepper again.

When Nolan and Pepper parted, his family hadn't kept their feelings about it to themselves...or rather their feelings about the reason why they parted. Nolan's defense had fallen on deaf ears. He'd been set with a plan of fulfilling his dream of becoming a surgeon, marrying Pepper and traveling with her during his off time.

But then they had lost the baby and their world had imploded around them.

"She's going to be living with me until this case is resolved."

Colt's brows shot up. "And you think this is all going to go that smoothly?"

"It has to."

Colt crossed his arms over his chest and shrugged. "You probably don't want my opinion—"

"Not at all."

"But you two haven't seen each other in years and you're already torn up. How do you think this fake marriage is going to play out?"

Good question, one he unfortunately had no clue how to answer. He hoped like hell he'd be working most of the time. Having Pepper so close yet so unobtainable would be pure torture. He wanted her with a desire that had nothing to do with the past and everything to do with the independent, beguiling woman she was today.

But she'd made it perfectly clear she wasn't interested. Did he actually believe she'd fall back into bed with him? No, but that didn't mean he wouldn't try. Everyone had a weakness and he fondly remembered every single one of hers.

"My house is big enough," Nolan explained. "And I've got double shifts coming up. I'd say for the most part we'll avoid each other."

Colt snorted and pushed off the door. "Keep telling yourself that, bro."

He would, because as much as he wanted to seduce his bride, he also knew she was vulnerable right now. He might be a doctor, but his bedside manner left something to be desired. He wasn't much on comforting or offering words of wisdom.

Added to that, there was too much at stake. Getting back in so deep with Pepper had potential to reopen old wounds he'd hoped would never be exposed again.

Something inside him had been damaged when Pepper left. If he had it to do over, he'd…hell, he didn't know what he'd do. They were both so different now, yet the familiarity…the aching want and need… was still simmering beneath the surface. Now they were thrown together, on borrowed time, but after this marriage they'd go back to being single. And he'd be in this big, empty home he'd built with no wife, no family. That was what he wanted, right?

Hadn't he said something to Pepper about a lonely life? He was the poster child.

Nolan rose to his feet. "Hayes will be home next week."

"I went by to see Dad earlier and told him. He was having a better day but wasn't sure who I was."

Their father was in and out of touch with reality—more out than in. But some days he recognized his sons. He often recalled their names but never put them with their faces.

"He remembered Hayes, but he thinks we're all in grade school," Colt added somberly.

"Maybe once Hayes goes to see Dad he will be having a good day. I'd hate for him to come home and catch him at a bad time for the first visit."

Hayes had been overseas for over a year now. He was finally getting out of the military and planning on farming for the time being. His house was back on the east side of the ranch and was the original Elliott home. It needed some renovations, but Nolan figured his brother would work on that as a way to keep busy because he wasn't the man he used to be. That much had been evident the last time he was home from a tour of duty.

"I've already blocked off some time next week," Nolan said. "I plan on being around more the first few days he's home."

"Good. He won't like us hovering, but he's always different when he's home and trying to acclimate back into the civilian world."

Colt fell into step beside his big brother as they headed out of the stable. "Did you come down to ride or to tell me about your marriage?"

"Both." Nolan pulled in a deep breath and glanced up at the orange-and-pink-streaked horizon. There was nothing like a sunset on the ranch. "But I'm going to head home. I can't keep avoiding this marriage."

Which meant neither could she.

Pepper had soaked in the oversize garden tub and enjoyed the wide window overlooking a portion of the ranch. Pebblebrook was the most beautiful piece of land she'd ever seen, and she'd done quite a bit of traveling.

She loved it all—the lush green grass, the brook winding through the property, the livestock dotting the horizon, the ever-present cowboys who worked here. The Elliott men were big, strong, handsome guys, but the stable hands were something to admire, too. They were in their forties, but farm life kept them in great shape.

Feeling more relaxed, Pepper slid into a simple sundress. She wouldn't mind continuing her evening of leisure by having some lemonade on the porch swing, but Nolan was around here somewhere. She wasn't quite sure she was ready to face him after that kiss.

If he didn't keep his hands and his lips off her, she didn't know if she'd be able to stop herself next time.

Pepper opted to take a stroll through the house instead. After all, shouldn't she get the lay of the land since she was now Mrs. Elliott? She wanted to see the finished product of their vision. They'd discussed so many details, yet this all seemed so new. Never once had she stopped to consider Nolan might actually go ahead with the plans they'd made.

When they'd played around with house designs, they'd discussed their future. Having kids had been a nebulous dream, but the realistic side of life had kicked them when she miscarried, ultimately driving an immovable wedge between them.

Pepper's heart tightened as she made her way down the wide hallway. Nervous about creeping through Nolan's house, she toyed with the foreign ring on her finger. Everything was so fresh yet so familiar. She'd seen these plans on paper, but had he changed much from their original vision?

She poked her head in the other bedrooms on this floor. They were all simply decorated in that muted, classy style. No doubt he'd hired a decorator to complete the home—a job she would've taken on had this been her place from day one. She would've splashed more color on the walls, accented with patterns and textures. And rugs. Mercy, this place needed some life.

After she closed the door on the last guest room, her eyes were drawn to the end of the hall where Nolan's master suite called to her. Her pulse quickened. Should she go inside? She had no rights here and he'd not given her the green light to explore.

Then again, she hadn't given him the go-ahead to kiss her, either, but he hadn't waited around for permission.

Squaring her shoulders, Pepper crossed the hall and didn't hesitate when her fingers closed over the knob. She turned it beneath her hand and opened the door. Her eyes instantly landed on the massive king-size bed occupying the middle of the floor, as if taking center stage.

A wide wall of windows with double doors in the middle to the patio took up the far wall. The room was identical to hers except for the layout of the decor and furniture.

An image of the two of them entangled in those sheets as they watched the sunrise flooded her mind.

Pepper moved farther into the room, transfixed by the fictitious scene. Her body responded, from memories of his touch or from the recent kiss, she wasn't sure. But this room smelled like him, all woodsy and masculine. The dark furniture screamed wealth and the navy bedding was so simple, yet she could see Nolan spread out with his sculpted shoulders and—

The bathroom door opened. Pepper jerked her gaze from the bed to the man in the steamy doorway. A man who wore nothing but dots of water glistening over taut skin stared back at her.

He propped one shoulder against the door frame as if he didn't care at all that he stood before her completely naked. Granted, Nolan had nothing to be ashamed of. If she'd thought that body was spectacular before, it was now a work of art.

"Decide to consummate the marriage after all?" he drawled.

His question pulled her attention back to his face. Her entire body heated at the way he stared back at her. So much raw desire and want and need, and with her hormones all over the place, she was barely hanging on.

"I—I was just looking around."

Nolan moved across the room, never taking his eyes off her. Pepper's heart kicked up as she tipped her head back to meet his gaze.

"In my bedroom, Pepper?" he asked in that low, husky tone.

There were too many things to take in all at once: the fresh, crisp scent from his shower, the heat that seemed to radiate off his bare body, the fact that said bare body was now inches from hers and the way he continued to look at her as if she were already his.

If he touched her now, she would not be responsible for her actions. She couldn't even lie to herself and pretend to be strong. No matter what her mind said, her heart yearned desperately for him.

"I was just looking around and—"

"When you say looking around, you mean at my bed? Because I saw your face. Were you daydreaming? Maybe about forgoing this agreement not to sleep together?"

Pepper willed herself to get control of this situation, but it was rather difficult when someone like Nolan was so…everything. He was overpowering, demanding in that confident, primal way.

"Whatever thoughts I have or don't have are none of your concern."

He trailed a fingertip up her bare arm, over her collarbone, and down the V of her dress. She couldn't suppress the tremble.

"I'd say they're very much my concern when I'm standing here naked and you're imagining yourself in my bed."

Eight

Nolan didn't care that he was pushing her. She'd stepped into his domain, so he considered her free game. Those wide eyes never wavered from his.

Undoubtedly he could spin her around and have her on his bed. He wasn't giving up on seduction, but he also wanted to be respectful. He'd ultimately started this marriage process as a way to give Pepper the family she'd always wanted. There was no point in rushing things. He had time to take her to bed because she wasn't going anywhere anytime soon.

"This was a mistake." She turned to go but stopped and glanced over her shoulder. "I'd rather do this on my own than have you mock me. Yes, I'm attracted to you—that was never our problem. So, if you want to revisit the past, I suggest you start opening up about why you abandoned me after all we'd been through."

Nolan didn't get a chance to respond before she strode from the room. He grabbed a pair of shorts that were folded on top of his dresser and hopped into them as he headed down the hall. He caught her bedroom door with a firm grip a second before she could slam it in his face.

"You want to talk about the past?" he said, storming into her room. "What do you want me to say, Pepper? That I handled things poorly? That I—"

She whirled around, her face flushed. "I don't know what I want! Apologizing won't change anything and I know we're different now, but…"

Pepper reached up and rubbed her forehead. The way she squeezed her eyes shut had Nolan rushing forward. She swayed slightly.

"Pepper."

She opened her eyes but didn't focus on him. Alarm shot through him, but that turned to full-on terror when she collapsed. He reached out just in time to keep her from falling to the floor.

The doctor in him kicked in, but the man who cared for her threatened to take over. What the hell had caused her to pass out? Was something wrong with the baby?

He scooped her up in his arms, then gently laid her down on her bed and smoothed her hair back from her face. Her face was still flushed and a sheen of perspiration covered her forehead. He rushed to the bathroom to get a cold cloth and then came back.

After placing it on her forehead, he checked her pulse. Strong and steady.

The stress must be getting to her. The fire, the custody issue…him. He hadn't made things exactly easy for her by goading her. If something happened to this child, Nolan would never forgive himself. *Pepper* would never forgive him.

Her lids fluttered, and Nolan eased down on the bed beside her. She opened her eyes and glanced around the room, then blinked and focused in on him.

"You passed out," he told her. "Don't try to move, darlin'. Just lie here a minute."

Her hands went to her stomach.

"I caught you," he informed her. "Have you fainted before with this pregnancy?"

"One other time," she admitted, taking the cloth from her head and attempting to sit up. "I'm okay. I think I just need to eat."

"You haven't had dinner? You can't be that careless at a time like this. You're already under too much pressure and that's not good for the baby."

She glared at him. "Really? I wasn't aware of the obvious."

Damn it. He was still panic-stricken and beside himself with worry from seeing her go down, and now she mocked him. Perfect. Just perfect. Wasn't this some wedding night to remember?

"No, I didn't eat. I took a bath to relax me and I was going to go downstairs and find something when I decided to take a tour."

"To my bedroom."

Her eyes turned to slits. "Your ego is out of control. I wasn't even aware you were home, so don't flatter yourself."

She might not have been aware he was home, but when he'd stepped out of his shower buck naked, she hadn't made a move to leave his room or to avert her eyes. That in itself spoke volumes.

"Stay here. I'll bring up something."

"I can get it."

Nolan stood up and stared sternly down at her. "No. You'll stay right here."

"I'm not playing the roll of the dutiful wife."

Placing a hand on either side of her hips, Nolan leaned down. "Darlin', you're far from dutiful where I'm concerned. But you're in no shape to go downstairs and cook. I'll get something quick and bring it back. Stop arguing."

As he turned to go, her softly spoken words stopped him. "Why are you doing this?"

He prided himself on being truthful when at all possible. Casting a glance over his shoulder, he replied gruffly, "Because I wasn't there for you before. This may not be my child, but I have to make it up to you somehow. I'm sorry I left you to handle the grief alone, but I'm trying to do right by you now."

"Actions from guilt won't erase the past," she countered.

"No, but I'll be damned if anything is going to happen to you or your baby. No matter what I have to pay for the custody dispute or how I have to care for you here, I'll do it."

He turned and walked out before he could say anything else that would betray his emotions. He wasn't quite sure what to even label them, but once words were said, they couldn't be taken back. So Nolan opted to remain quiet and concentrate instead on caring for her.

Pepper was his wife, which meant right now her child was his. No, not literally, but in his view, they were his to care for, to protect. This wasn't the best mind-set to be in, but considering the choices that had been made thus far, this was where he stood. He couldn't deny he wanted her with him. And that went beyond merely wanting to shield her from harm. He wanted to see if that old spark, the one that still simmered between them, was real.

He already knew the answer to that.

Maybe he should take some time off in addition to the days next week. He had more than enough saved up and with Hayes coming home from overseas, now would be a good time to take a break. Besides, someone needed to look after Pepper, whether she wanted to admit it or not. And, heaven help him, he was the only man for the job.

Five days had passed since she'd fainted and she'd purposely taken better care of herself. She didn't want to rely on Nolan any more than necessary.

He'd worked the next three days and then informed her he'd be off. Wonderful. Just what she needed. Time alone with her husband wasn't something she was exactly looking forward to. The temptation was much too strong.

As Pepper pulled into the drive of her temporary home, she glanced to the black-and-white images lying in her passenger seat. Images of her baby boy.

Nothing could spoil this day. She'd been counting down the days till she found out the sex of her baby. Now that it was confirmed she was having a boy, she wanted to focus on getting ready for her son's arrival. A wave of anticipation rippled through her as she envisioned getting back to her apartment and setting up a fun nursery with paintings she'd done herself. Maybe she'd put a mural on the wall over his crib.

But then reality set in. The contractor wasn't done with her apartment and she wasn't going to be living there anytime soon anyway. She'd yet to hear from the attorney and everything in her hoped the Wrights would just drop this case.

That was wishful thinking.

Colt led his horse from the stable as she passed by. Since she made eye contact, she threw up a hesitant hand in an awkward wave as she drove on. Odd to just wave as if they were truly family or friends. She hadn't had a face-to-face conversation with him since being here. Granted, he was busy and, well, she was doing everything she could to avoid bumping into her husband.

She stayed after at her shop to paint and make new arrangements to replace some that had sold. So far Painted Pansies was thriving. Mostly people strolled through to see what the new shop had to offer, which was fine. She hoped they'd come back and tell their friends, drumming up more business.

Maybe she should plan an open house. Something after hours for those who worked. Definitely something to consider. A glimmer of hope coursed through her for the first time since she'd moved in. She knew that focusing on positive aspects of her life was what would help her get through this tumultuous time.

Eventually she would have her life just the way she'd dreamed. But she had to tread carefully here because giving in to her attraction to Nolan would only derail her plans.

Pepper parked in the driveway and went into the house through the garage door. All of Nolan's vehicles were in the garage, but that didn't mean he was home. He often went out on his horse or four-wheeler and lately he'd been at Hayes's house making sure everything was ready for his brother's return. She preferred when he was out because he tended to hover whenever he was nearby. Not that she was unappreciative…he had truly gone above and beyond to make her feel comfortable. He had his chef come in every other day to make up meals so Pepper didn't have to do a thing. She even had lunches prepared so Pepper could take them to work.

Nolan had thought of everything, but they'd still not resumed their heated conversation from the other day. Would he apologize for how he'd treated her? He was obviously a different man now. Perhaps becoming a doctor had changed him, or maybe her leaving had. Of course, that was her broken heart talking.

When she'd left, she'd waited for him to reach out, to call her back and tell her they'd work through everything and they'd be all right. That never happened and she'd finally had to push through the pain and realize that life without Nolan was her new reality. She'd made plans without him—she wouldn't upend them again. Doing so would only end in more heartache for her and her child.

Pepper hung her purse on the hook near the back door and clutched her baby's pictures in the other hand. Maybe she could get a little frame to put them in. She couldn't wait to see her son's sweet face in person and cuddle him in her arms.

The back patio door opened and Nolan stepped in. The spacious kitchen and eat-in breakfast area separated them, but those bright eyes still zeroed right in on her.

"You're getting home pretty late," he commented as he yanked his hat off and wiped his forehead with the back of his hand.

Pepper straightened her back and tipped her chin. "I wasn't aware you were keeping tabs."

"My contractor called and said you'd talked to him when you left the shop almost two hours ago."

She moved farther into the kitchen and stopped at the large center island. "Well, I had something to do after work. I already told you going into this marriage that it was on paper only. I'm still my own boss."

He propped his hat back on his head and crossed the room, coming to stand across from her. His gaze drifted to the ultrasound images in her hand.

"You were at the doctor?"

Pepper nodded.

"I would've gone with you."

Surprised he'd even mention such a thing, she merely shrugged. "Didn't cross my mind to mention it. That's not something you ever wanted to do before."

The muscles in his jaw ticked as he continued to look at the pictures. "We've already established I'm a different man."

"A man who wants kids in his life?"

Those bright blues came up to meet her gaze as silence surrounded them.

"That's what I thought," she finally murmured.

He reached across and slid the pictures from her hand. As he unfolded the long strip of paper, he studied the ultrasound shots.

"A boy," he muttered. "Congratulations."

"Thank you."

He laid the photos back on the counter and looked at her again. "I heard from my lawyer today. We have a meeting set up for tomorrow morning with the Wrights and their attorney."

Fear clutched her heart. "I was hoping they were going to let this drop."

Nolan came around the counter and took her hands in his, forcing her to face him. "No matter what you and I have been through, or how we feel now, I won't let your child get taken away. I've got the best attorney in the state on this and I'll call in a whole damn team if need be. Let me handle this, Pepper. You focus on your baby boy."

In theory that sounded nice, but in reality this was her battle to fight. Unfortunately, she didn't have near the impressive bank account that Nolan did. So as much as she wanted to stand on her own two feet, right now she needed his help. She just wished it hadn't come at such a high price.

Why did he have to seem so caring, so concerned with her emotions? She couldn't emotionally afford to have him so invested. Financially, she'd take all he could offer in order to keep her child, but anything too intimate or personal could possibly destroy her once all was said and done. Because in the end, they would part ways.

"I just want all of this to be over," she told him, not caring that she was vulnerable. There was only so long a person could be strong and she was almost at her breaking point.

"It will be soon and then you can get on with your life," he assured her as he cupped her cheek, stroking his thumb across her skin.

He sounded so confident and she hoped he was right. If she only had an ounce of his certainty, it would go a long way in easing her mind.

But with the impending meeting in the morning, there would be no relaxing until she saw what she was up against. Maybe after talking with Nolan's attorney herself, she'd get a clearer picture.

She sighed despite herself. As hard as it was to admit, the fact that Nolan insisted on coming with her and sticking by her throughout this entire ordeal filled her with a measure of comfort. She wished she could be angry with him, but how could she? Yes, he'd treated her badly years ago, but he was truly trying to make up for it now. Pepper knew he still cared or he wouldn't be going to so much trouble. Even with his guilt, there was a level of concern and it warmed her, made her wonder what type of man he was now.

And maybe she wanted to get to know this Nolan a bit better. The prospect seemed terrifying. The risk to all of this temptation was almost more than she could bear. But the intrigue was there...and she'd already been pulled in too far to back out now.

Nine

"I didn't know you used to live in Montana and Oregon."

The meeting with the attorneys and the Wrights had gone about as abysmally as he'd thought it would. Nolan had sat by Pepper's side as everyone discussed the custody of her unborn child. The more he listened, the more he realized the Wrights were indeed going to fight dirty.

Their attorney brought up Pepper's frequent moves over the past ten years. The only upside to the whole debacle was that Nolan discovered quite a bit about her, courtesy of their extensive background check, and appreciated the insight to her life. Although, he wasn't too keen on the way they made her sound so unstable. Having known her for years, he understood the way she used the adventure as a way to cope with her grief.

"Both were beautiful states." She continued to stare out the window of his SUV as he headed toward her shop because she insisted on working. "Other than Texas, I think Oregon was my favorite place to live."

"You love it here?" he asked, surprised.

Pepper shifted in her seat, smoothing a hand down her pregnant belly. "What's not to love? The small-town feel with the big-city attractions. All of the farms, the old homes, and the architecture. Not to mention all the little shops and parks. Stone River is a beautiful town."

He gripped the wheel tighter. "Would you have stayed?"

Silence settled heavy between them. He should've kept his mouth shut and not said a word. But he'd always wondered. If she hadn't gotten pregnant, had a miscarriage…if he hadn't acted like a jerk because he was overcome with grief, would she have stayed? Would they be living in his house on Pebblebrook for real as a married couple?

"I would've done anything for you," she murmured.

Nolan swallowed the lump of remorse. He believed her. She'd have stayed even though she wanted to go travel the world. He hadn't been able to see it at the time, but now he knew the truth. She'd have done anything to make him happy, to stay together. He was the one who hadn't held up his part of the commitment.

Relationships weren't always fifty-fifty, with each person giving fully of themselves—a life fact he'd discovered the hard way. At least, that was what his father had always said, and Nolan's parents had had an extremely successful marriage.

He didn't even think before he reached across and slid his hand over hers. "I'm sorry that was difficult back there."

"Not your fault." Pepper blew out a sigh and changed the subject. "I think we stunned them with the marriage announcement."

Nolan smiled. "That was the idea."

They'd explained that Pepper had come back to her hometown because she and Nolan had reconnected. Not a total lie. Nolan had stayed by her side, offering her support and comfort as she was given the third degree on why she moved so much, why she held so many jobs and why she thought this new venture into entrepreneurship would be the thing to keep her grounded.

The fact that he was a doctor didn't seem to impress the Wrights. If anything, they looked ready to attack him, too. Nolan didn't care what they did. His record as a surgeon was impeccable. He was the top general surgeon in the entire state and if they had the balls to dig into his financial records, they'd find he could buy them out five times over if he wanted.

So, no, he wasn't afraid of them and he hoped like hell they knew who they were up against, because they were going to lose.

"I have to go into the hospital," he told her as he turned into the lot behind Painted Pansies. "The next three days will be busy. I have twelve-hour shifts, so don't look for me at home during normal hours."

Pepper gathered up her purse from the floorboard. "Does a doctor even have such a thing as normal hours?"

"Not at all," he chuckled. "I'll have a couple of the ranch hands drop your car off to you so you can get back home."

He pulled up to the back door and before she could get out, he squeezed her hand to get her attention. "I wasn't lying when I told you everything would be all right."

Her dark eyes met his. "I want to believe that."

The way she looked at him, with so much hope, twisted something deep inside him. Yeah, he'd slay all her dragons, but then he couldn't help but wonder if he'd be battling himself. His hands were dirty, too, when it came to hurting Pepper.

"Will you be okay at the house alone? You remember how the alarm system works?"

Pepper nodded. "I'll be fine."

Damn it. For the first time since he became a doctor, he actually dreaded going into work. But he knew he had a full schedule of surgeries and there were always emergencies that occurred with patients.

"I don't like leaving you."

That revelation came as quick as the words spilled from his mouth. He wanted to spend more time with her, and that was a dangerous thought.

Pepper's brows rose. Yeah, he caught the irony in that statement, too, but he meant it.

"Promise me you'll eat regular meals," he ordered.

"I can take care of myself, Nolan."

She tugged her hand free, and he hated the lost connection. He didn't want her to withdraw. He wanted her to hold on to him, to allow him to gather her close and soothe her worries away. How could he continue to help her if she insisted on guarding her heart? He couldn't blame her, but damn it, he was trying. He wasn't going to stop reaching for her, touching her, kissing her.

"Pepper…"

She gripped her purse in her lap. "I really need to get the shop open. I promise everything will be fine."

Unable to stop himself, he leaned across the console, curled his fingers around the back of her neck, and brought her mouth to his. He brushed his lips over hers, shocked when she parted for him.

Threading his fingers through the hair at the nape of her neck, Nolan tipped his head to capture more of her.

The kiss was quick yet left him wanting more as he eased back just slightly. Part of him wanted to keep kissing her, but he refrained. Maybe if he kept giving her a taste of what they could have, she'd come to him of her own accord. He knew he could have her begging.

"What was that for?" she breathed against his mouth.

"I won't deny myself what I want anymore."

Her body trembled beneath his touch. "And that includes me?"

He nipped at her lips once more before releasing

her. "Have a good day at work and don't hesitate to call Colt if you need something. He knows I'm working and he's right there on the property."

Pepper stared at him. No, he wasn't answering her question; she already knew what he'd say. Hell, yes, she was included in that statement. He wanted her—he knew it was unsettling, risky, but he'd eventually have her in his bed…or wherever else he could take her.

Both times he'd kissed her, she'd melted against him and kissed right back. There was no reason they had to deny themselves what they both wanted.

"You're making this difficult for me," she stated as she opened her door. "If you want to kiss me, fine. But don't push, Nolan. I'm not strong enough to fight for my baby and resist you, too."

She hopped out of the SUV and headed to the back door of Painted Pansies.

Well, damn. If that didn't give him hope, nothing would. She was just as achy as he was. He knew Pepper and there was no way a woman that passionate would be able to resist him. Not that he was God's gift to women—he wasn't that arrogant. But he wasn't naive, either. They had unfinished business between them whether she was willing to admit it or not.

A smile played on his lips. Pepper had no clue that after these three days were over, he'd be home for a bit. He never took vacation and with Hayes coming home, Nolan wanted to be there.

Maybe he'd just surprise her.

Nolan pulled away as soon as Pepper was safely inside. Yeah, he'd surprise her. Wouldn't she just love that?

After having the ranch to herself for a few days, Pepper had completed and sold several paintings with six to spare and had a few rather profitable days at the shop. With each customer who came through, she had to explain the noises overhead. All of the hammering and sawing was music to her ears, however. Most of the townsfolk knew of the fire and were quite sympathetic, which added to sales.

As soon as she got out of this awkward marriage, Pepper planned to be back in her building, where she could live and work while raising her baby. Because *she* would be the one to raise her son—there was no other option as far as she was concerned. Having strangers get custody wasn't even a possibility she wanted to entertain.

For now, she needed to remain as calm as possible if she wanted to keep her blood pressure under control. Her son's health came first. Everything she was doing was for him. Through each step of this pregnancy, she'd had fears. So many memories of her first pregnancy swirled around in her mind, the roller coaster of emotions from the excitement to the anger, then the loss and the emptiness—the broken heart.

Pepper stepped back and tipped her head to the side as she examined the new painting she'd done last night when she couldn't sleep. Between her demanding pregnancy bladder and all the worries of the future, she'd barely gotten a few hours. And that wasn't even touching on all the swirling thoughts in her head regarding her new husband.

Once she'd started painting, she'd become lost in the moment. The soft strokes of coral and pale gray looked so much better in Nolan's living room of navy and white. That old ugly black-and-white picture he had really needed to go. He might be a bachelor—or he used to be—but that didn't mean he had to live in a constant state of bore.

Pepper had already put a bright watercolor painting in her bedroom. She needed the yellows and oranges to brighten up all the beige. *Beige.* Who the hell chose that color to decorate with? Why be so mundane?

So far she'd added three paintings to his home, and the third one was propped on his dresser in his bedroom. Also a dark, somber room done in navy and dark wood, so she went with something bold and bright to spruce things up. Various shades of reds and golds ought to make his domain a happier place.

Not that she figured he'd say anything. A man like Nolan didn't care about decor, because she knew him well enough to know he'd hired interior designers to have his home done but he'd most likely told them to keep it neutral.

Neutral. Just the word made her cringe. If she'd lived here from the beginning, the words *beige* and *gray* wouldn't even have been in the mix. Each room would've been its own showpiece. There was so much possibility to liven things up, but this wasn't really her house and she couldn't exactly transform everything. But a few of her one-of-a-kind paintings couldn't hurt.

The furniture and decor all over the house had been chosen with a man in mind—dominant, bold, rich.

From the automatic lights and blinds to the indoor-and-outdoor pool and even a megatheater room, everything was so grand. He had deviated slightly from their master plans years ago, but only to make this place even more larger-than-life. Because when they'd first tinkered around with house plans, they'd still been in that dreamy stage of their love affair. Pepper never actually thought she'd have a master suite with a sweeping balcony to overlook the land but it sure had been fun fantasizing about it.

Dreaming with Nolan had been her favorite hobby when she was twenty years old. Making love by the brook that ran through the ranch had been another of their favorite pastimes. With an estate this vast, there were plenty of areas to find privacy for young lovers.

It wasn't difficult to imagine her life here. Had she not miscarried, she and Nolan would've still built this amazing home on his family's estate. She wondered how he lived here all alone, though. Did he even go in half the rooms of this massive home? Had he thought of her as he built this place? As he designed the master suite?

No. She wasn't going to get caught up in the fantasy life she could've had or the fact that she still craved Nolan. He may be different than the boy she left behind, but he was also very much the same. And try as she might, she still wanted his touch, even if it was only temporary.

Pepper padded barefoot back through the house, the dark hardwood floor smooth beneath her feet. A gentle kick in her belly had her rubbing a hand over her tank top and smiling. She loved every moment of feeling her little boy move. Every time he shifted, she wanted to freeze that moment. As excited as she was to hold him, she would miss this wondrous feeling.

She headed back to the living room and surveyed the three paintings still waiting to find a home. She could put them in the shop, but she already had so many and she didn't want the small retail space to look cluttered.

"What the hell are you doing?"

Pepper swiveled around, her hand over her chest as her heart quickened at the intrusion. Nolan stood behind her with his hands on his hips. Dark hair all disheveled, lips set in a thin, hard line and jaw clenched, he was clearly pissed about something.

"I didn't hear you come in," she stated breathlessly. "Care to tell me why you're angry with me?"

His hand gestured toward the painting over his fireplace, then to the ones resting to the side. "Are you redecorating?"

So much for him not noticing. "I, uh, thought—"

"Did you think about the paint chemicals?" he added, his voice rising.

Pepper had no idea what had put him in this mood, but she didn't have to stick around to listen. "I use the best paints and in a ventilated area. I also have a mask I wear, not that it's any of your concern," she huffed. "And if you hate it so much, I can easily take down the paintings and put your boring, lifeless art back in place. It's clear some things never change. Whatever Nolan wants, Nolan gets."

She turned on her heel, marched across the room and carefully lifted the painting from the nail. With unshed tears, she cursed herself for getting too comfortable. Over the past three days she'd been alone here, she'd begun to think of this as her place...which was a terrible mistake.

Firm hands gripped her arms, and Pepper stiffened as she gripped the painting. "Don't," she whispered. "I don't want to argue."

And she didn't want to see that look in his eyes again, the one that was clearly disapproving of her getting too cozy in his home.

Ten

Nolan didn't mean to take his piss-poor mood out on Pepper, but he'd just been totally caught off guard. He was used to coming home to a quiet, empty house after work, unwinding by riding his horse Doc or hitting his workout room with the punching bag and free weights. Plus, he'd nearly lost a patient tonight and he was still turned inside out about the whole ordeal. He'd lost patients before, but now that Pepper had come back into his life, this particular experience only made him remember so vividly the time when they'd lost their baby.

"I didn't expect to come in here and see that you'd redecorated," he explained in a milder tone, as if that somehow made up for the way he'd greeted her. "Something wrong with my artwork?"

FREE Merchandise is 'in the Cards' for you!

Dear Reader,

We're giving away FREE MERCHANDISE!

Seriously, we'd like to reward you for reading this novel by giving you **FREE MERCHANDISE** worth over **$20** retail. And no purchase is necessary!

You see the Jack of Hearts sticker above? Paste that sticker in the box on the Free Merchandise Voucher inside. Return the Voucher today... and we'll send you Free Merchandise!

Thanks again for reading one of our novels—and enjoy your Free Merchandise with our compliments!

Pam Powers

Pam Powers

P.S. Look inside to see what Free Merchandise is **"in the cards"** for you!

W

e'd like to send you two free books like the one you are enjoying now. Your two books have a combined cover price of over $10 retail, but they are yours to keep absolutely FREE! We'll even send you 2 wonderful surprise gifts. You can't lose!

REMEMBER: Your Free Merchandise, consisting of **2 Free Books** and **2 Free Gifts**, is worth over $20 retail! No purchase is necessary, so please send for your Free Merchandise today.

Get TWO FREE GIFTS!

We'll also send you 2 wonderful FREE GIFTS (worth about $10 retail), in addition to your 2 Free books!

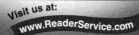

Visit us at:
www.ReaderService.com

Books received may not be as shown.

FREE MERCHANDISE VOUCHER

> **2 FREE BOOKS and 2 FREE GIFTS**

Please send my Free Merchandise, consisting of **2 Free Books** and **2 Free Mystery Gifts**. I understand that I am under no obligation to buy anything, as explained on the back of this card.

225/326 HDL GLTD

Please Print

FIRST NAME

LAST NAME

ADDRESS

APT.#   CITY

STATE/PROV.   ZIP/POSTAL CODE

NO PURCHASE NECESSARY!

HD-517-FM17

Reluctantly, he released her so she could turn to face him. When she didn't, Nolan curled his fingers around her shoulders and eased her around. There was a tiredness in her eyes, one that he hadn't seen before...one he didn't want to see again.

No matter what he'd been through on this last shift, Pepper came first. His *wife* and this child had to take top priority. At this point he wasn't even questioning why he'd allowed this faux family to overtake his life. There were too many reasons to list—and none he wanted to address.

"Your walls are boring." She raised her chin up in defiance, as if silently daring him to argue. "I'm sure you paid a ridiculous price to have this place decorated, but it's putting me to sleep."

He didn't even try to stop himself as he reached out to swipe the pad of his thumb beneath her eye. "You're not sleeping enough."

She blinked, her long lashes brushing against the tip of his thumb. Cupping her cheek, he felt his chest tighten when she leaned just slightly into him.

"I'm in a new place," she explained, those dark gray eyes holding his. "I'm trying to adjust to my surroundings."

"You've traveled all over and adjusted. Why can't you just put your feet up and relax?"

Pepper offered a soft smile. "You know the answer to that."

Yeah, he knew. The same reason he'd been so worked up about coming home, knowing he'd be off for the next few days…which he still hadn't informed her of.

"Have you heard from anyone regarding the case?" he asked, dropping his hand but remaining close enough to touch.

She shook her head. "Not a word, hence all the new paintings."

Nolan couldn't help but smile as he glanced to the new addition to his living room. "You always painted when you were nervous or worried."

He recalled a few times when they'd been dating and she'd gotten anxious about something, no matter how minor. Some people reached for pills to combat anxiety—his Pepper reached for her paintbrush.

"I did more than the six I brought home," she stated with a shrug. "I put several in the shop and most of them sold."

"That's great." He was so proud of her for opening her shop and already showing that she was going to make it successful. "Business has been good, then?"

He suppressed a smile. Okay, so he *may* have been chatting up her new shop a bit to folks at work. He'd mentioned it casually to his male coworkers in case they needed flowers or a gift and had also told several of the ladies in his department where they could find one-of-a-kind paintings.

"Better than I'd expected, but I know that will die down once the novelty wears off."

Nolan glanced to the stack of canvases on the ottoman. He crossed the room and lifted one up to examine the colors. The vibrant image seemed to jump out at him and he looked closer at the fine details she'd added to each stroke. The variations of tones, then the bold shades that demanded attention.

"I doubt the novelty wears off," he returned as he laid that piece aside to survey the other two. "These are extraordinary."

Nolan turned back around, surprised to see a slight blush creep up her cheeks. "You have to know how talented you are."

"It all started as a way to relax and take my mind away from reality. I know I have a gift, but when I hear someone I care about tell me…"

Her eyes widened as she jerked her gaze to his. Yeah, he'd caught that slip. Apparently she didn't want him to know just how much she still cared or that declaration wouldn't bother her so much.

At least he wasn't the only one worried about what to say or how to act.

He strode across the room, never taking his eyes from hers. "We have to have complete honesty, Pepper. I know you care for me. I could feel it when you kissed me."

"You kissed me," she corrected.

"And I plan on doing it again." As often as he could, actually. "But my stance hasn't changed since you were here last. I'm not looking for a family."

Pepper folded her arms over her chest, which only aided in pushing her breasts up. He wouldn't be so trite as to stare, but damn, she looked good.

"And you think that because I'm staying here, I won't be able to resist throwing myself at you?" she asked, her tone mocking. "In case you didn't know, I have quite a bit on my plate at the moment. As much as your ego would love for me to fawn all over you, you're not high on my priority list. And as for more kissing? That's not a good idea."

Nolan moved toward her, pleased when her eyes widened. When his chest brushed against her forearms, she immediately dropped her arms to her sides.

"None of this is a good idea, yet here we are."

Those dark flecks in her eyes drew him in. She was an enigma and he was fighting a losing battle... even so, he couldn't surrender. They were different people now. If she hadn't come back and turned his life on its head, he'd still be going along just like he always had. And he was just fine with that...wasn't he?

"You didn't have to marry me," she reminded him. "This was your idea. I would've found a way to keep custody of my baby."

"I'm sure you would've, but this way is easier."

Pepper's laugh filled the room. "Easier? Being married to you and living in a house we designed is definitely *not* easier. I'm temporarily living the only real dream I ever had and I know in a short time, it will all be ripped from me once again."

Nolan clenched his jaw as he reached for her. Settling his hands on her shoulders, he forced himself to face this emotional beast head-on.

"This isn't the same as before," he countered.

Pepper nodded. "You're right. I'm going in with my eyes wide-open. I know the outcome. I appreciate all you're doing for me, Nolan, but every bit of this stings and I can't help how I feel. You wanted honesty, and that's it. Being here with you is hard."

Since they'd first seen each other only days ago, things had become so intense so fast. He needed to lighten the moment, to show her that they could live together and get through this without always throwing the past out in the open like a weapon.

"Are you too tired to go somewhere?" he asked.

Pepper's brows drew in as she gave him the side eye. "Depends on where."

"The old Pepper wouldn't question me. She'd just jump at the unknown and the idea of an adventure."

With a soft smile, she let out a sigh. "Fine. Lead the way, but nothing too adventurous. I'm carrying precious cargo these days."

As if he could forget. That rounded stomach, her new voluptuous figure, the reason they'd married... and the fact this was another man's baby.

Nolan had to face the truth that the crux of his entire bad mood lately was that fact alone. Jealousy had never been an issue with him, but Pepper was different. She was special.

And eventually, that was going to be a problem because these weren't past feelings he was having. Everything he craved now was the new Pepper, this vibrant woman who was made of steel yet had such a vulnerable interior.

Nolan took her hand and led her from the house. The sooner they eased the stress and relaxed, the better. There was a fine line he was hanging on to...and it was about ready to snap.

* * *

Pepper entered the dark stables and waited at the doorway while Nolan stepped in and flicked on the lights. She couldn't suppress the gasp. She hadn't forgotten the beauty of the old stone barn, but she'd been gone so long the place had been out of her mind.

The stone pathway leading between the stalls stretched to the other end of the stables. Each stable was separated by sturdy, thick wood beams and an occasional worn wooden bench. Old industrial wheels had been turned into modern chandeliers that were suspended from the vaulted beams.

There was no expense spared on this masterpiece and the horses were no different. Pepper knew the Elliotts kept only the best stock. They offered stud services, as well. Everything about this farm, from the horses to the men, dominated. There was no denying Pebblebrook Ranch was remarkable.

Nolan turned back to her. He'd transformed from a doctor in scrubs to a cowboy complete with Stetson and tight jeans in the span of minutes. Now he stood before her so much like the boy she used to know. But Nolan was all man, filling out his dark blue shirt with muscles that nearly pulled at the seams.

"I know you're not supposed to ride, but I thought you might like to see what we have. You always used to love coming down here."

She had. And every time they'd come down, they'd ended up in the loft overhead. There was nothing sexy about the smell of a stable or the straw on your back, but when she was with Nolan, nothing else had mattered.

Over the years she'd imagined him here, tending to the horses, working on this beloved ranch. This was his life and he was good at it. A burst of jealousy speared through her that she hadn't shared this part of his life when she'd dreamed for so long of being here.

The baby stirred in her belly, and Pepper placed both hands over her bump, wanting to capture every single moment.

Nolan's eyes dropped to her stomach. "Is he moving?"

Pepper nodded, reaching for him. "Want to feel?"

His gaze jerked to hers as he stilled. This entire situation was so foreign to her she had no idea how to react. But she couldn't lie that disappointment didn't spiral through her. She really had no one else to share these joyful moments with. And not that Nolan was her real husband or even her best friend, but he was here... He'd volunteered to be here. She just wished...

Did it matter? She'd had so many wishes over the years and she should know by now that none of them came true.

"It's okay." Pepper offered a smile she wasn't quite feeling. "I didn't mean to make you uncomfortable."

The awkward silence had Pepper smoothing her tank down her belly, causing her bangles to clang against each other. She took a step to move around Nolan and head toward the stalls. Before she could take the second step, however, his big hand snaked out, landing on her abdomen, stopping her instantly.

That strong, warm palm made Pepper's breath catch in her throat. Tipping her head to the side, she met those deep blue eyes beneath his black hat. He turned slightly, placing both hands over her abdomen as he kept his eyes locked on to hers.

Pepper didn't move, didn't breathe. Nolan had completely mesmerized her by his sheer masculine power, his silent command for her to let him do this. And she wanted his hands on her. She wanted him to be part of her life, not in the temporary way, either. There was no lying to herself anymore. She was growing more attracted to Nolan. Her need for him had nothing to do with the past and everything to do with the man he was today.

"He's an active little guy." Nolan's smile widened as he glanced down to his hands. "Is he always like this?"

"Lately. It almost feels like he's flipping at times, but I know he's not. My ultrasound showed he's exactly where he should be and his heart rate is perfect. He's the size of a can of soda."

Nolan laughed. "Amazing."

"I'd think a doctor wouldn't find something like this so remarkable."

Nolan's hands shifted when the baby slowed. He searched for the movement, but Pepper wasn't about to tell him the baby had stopped wiggling.

"I don't deal with babies and definitely not pregnant women. But even if I did, you're different. You could never be just a patient to me."

Pulling in a deep breath, Pepper closed her eyes

and willed herself to remain in control. Part of her
wanted to give in to the weakness and throw her arms
around him, lean into him and let him carry her over
this life hurdle.

But the independent woman inside her demanded
she deal with this head-on. There was no future here,
so there was no reason in letting her mind, or her
heart, wander into forbidden territory.

"You can't say things like that to me." She opened
her eyes and backed away slightly. "Now, show me
your horses, because I've missed this simple life."

He didn't move; he just continued to stare at her
as if seeing her for the first time.

"You're beautiful like this," he murmured huskily.
"Fuller figure, hair down, desire in your eyes. I always pictured you back here. I wondered if you'd
ever return."

Pepper's heart clenched with each word. Marrying
him might have sounded like the perfect solution in
theory, but now that reality had set in, she wasn't sure
she could continue. She wanted too much.

Before she could tell him they needed to keep focused on why they were forced together, Nolan closed
the narrow space between them. His boots shuffled
against the stone, breaking the tense silence.

"Tell me you haven't thought of us since you left."

Pepper's resolve crumbled as he loomed over her,
looking down into her eyes with such…raw desire.

"Nolan—"

"Tell me," he demanded. "I see how you look at

me. I feel you trembling now beneath my touch. You want me as much as I want you."

She did, but her feelings, her *wants*, didn't matter.

"I want you," she admitted, not surprised when her voice cracked. "I thought of you, of this ranch, every day for years. But then everything faded. I moved on. You moved on, too."

Banding an arm around her waist, he thrust his other hand into her hair and tilted her head back. "Or maybe we haven't."

Nolan captured her mouth, sending every single doubt and red flag to the back of her mind. In the fury of motions, his hat fell with a soft thump to the ground.

All Pepper could feel, all she could concentrate on, was this potent man who overtook every single emotion.

His hard body lined up perfectly with hers—just like she remembered. Even with her baby bump, it was like they were made for each other...and part of her still believed they were.

Nolan gripped her hair, pulling just enough to send another burst of arousal through her. Not only was he commanding, he knew exactly what it took to turn her on.

Pepper grasped his biceps and returned the kiss, opening further for him. She couldn't deny herself this pleasure. Didn't want to. She'd already had so much taken from her and for these few stolen moments, she was going to be selfish and damn the consequences.

Nolan tore his mouth from hers to rain kisses along her jaw, down the column of her throat. Pepper arched her back, giving him full access. He tugged at the scoop in her tank, managing to pull her bra to the side, as well, exposing one breast. When his lips closed over her heated skin, Pepper cried out and reached up to clutch the sides of his head.

Her entire body lit up from within. But if she didn't put a stop to this, there was no question where they were heading. She tingled all over and it was difficult for her to remember why this wasn't the smartest move.

"Nolan." Why did his name come out like a pant? Maybe one more minute, that was all she needed. Then she'd stop him.

Those talented lips traveled back up until he feasted on her mouth once again. Pepper pressed herself against him, needing to feel more, wanting to rid herself of these clothes and—

No. That was exactly the opposite of what she should want.

She pushed away from Nolan and his spellbinding kiss. As she took a step back, then another for good measure, she tugged her tank up and made sure she was fully covered before she looked him in the eye.

But when she did, there was so much staring back at her. Beyond all the passion and arousal, though, was one emotion worrying her most. Determination. She knew without a shadow of a doubt that Nolan wasn't done with her, that this was only the beginning…and she'd let this happen. She'd wanted it.

"Don't say anything." His stroked his thumb across her bottom lip. "You're not sorry this happened and you don't regret it. You can't lie to me, darlin'. I can see everything in your eyes."

That was precisely what she was afraid of. It never mattered what she said or did—her eyes always revealed the truth.

"Maybe I'm not sorry and I don't regret it," she told him, trying to ignore that tingle shooting through her. "But at this point in my life, I am not looking to revisit the past or even get swept into an affair."

"I'm your husband."

As if she could forget. The unfamiliar band on her finger was a constant reminder of the decision she'd made in order to attempt to secure her baby's future.

"In name only." The reminder wasn't just for Nolan. "I know a man like you…"

Smoothing her hair away from her face, Nolan flashed her a naughty grin. "A man like me? Please, keep going."

"A healthy, virile man will find this difficult, but we can't… I can't…"

He covered her mouth, softly, possessively, with his. Feathering his lips over hers, he rendered her speechless once again. Pepper turned her head, causing his lips to land on her cheek.

No matter if his kisses were rough and demanding or soft and sweet, Nolan had the same impact on her as if he'd stripped her bare. The man was too potent and she was sinking deeper and deeper into a place she feared she'd never recover from.

"Did you bring me down here to seduce me?" she whispered.

His warm breath fanned her skin, causing even more chills to course through her. "Baby, when I seduce you, I won't worry about the location."

Pepper filled her lungs and turned around, taking a minute to gather her thoughts. Her body betrayed her because she wanted nothing more than to whirl back around and have Nolan finish what he'd started.

She rested a hand over her belly as her son shifted. The reminder was all she needed. He came first; nothing else mattered. Not the past, not her present internal battles…nothing.

Pepper glanced over her shoulder. "Are we going back to the house or are we here to see the horses?"

Nolan's deep gaze was just as potent as his touch, but Pepper raised a brow, silently informing him she was in charge.

Nolan reached out, grabbed her hand, and led her toward the farthest stall. But Pepper still didn't let her guard down. As long as he insisted on touching her, she was going to have to keep giving herself pep talks. Nolan was a force to be reckoned with… and he knew it.

"This is Doc."

Nolan pointed to the stallion with deep chocolate eyes and a glossy chestnut coat. He was absolutely beautiful. Pepper reached for him, running her fingertips along his velvety nose.

"He's magnificent," she murmured. With his head

tilted slightly, Doc seemed as if he was looking right at her. "He's a gentle horse."

"He is," Nolan agreed, patting the stallion's neck. "We understand each other. I ride him every day that I'm off. Sometimes I need a longer ride to decompress, but on occasion I take him out and see what he can do."

Pepper smiled, glancing to Nolan. "You take turns being in charge."

Adjusting his hat, he let out a bark of laughter. "I suppose, though he thinks he's always in charge."

"Much like his owner?" she quipped, turning to face him. "Sounds like you two are a perfect match."

The fans blowing through the stable sent Pepper's hair stirring around her shoulders, just slightly, but enough to tickle her bare skin. She reached back and fisted it, pulling the thick strands over one shoulder. Nolan remained quiet as he seemed to be taking in every move she made.

When the silence became too much, she stilled. "What?"

"You look good here at Pebblebrook."

The soft tone, the way the muscles in his jaw clenched, Pepper knew he hadn't meant to let that slip out. She tried not to allow the words to penetrate her heart, but how could she not? She'd gotten a sneak peek into his most private thoughts.

"I haven't brought another woman here." He continued stroking Doc's neck, then patted his head before he resumed stroking again. "Never seemed right."

Pepper wasn't sure what he wanted her to say, so she kept quiet. She wasn't going to deny that knowing he hadn't brought other women here thrilled her. She had no right to those emotions, but she could always blame it on the pregnancy hormones…right?

"What are you doing tomorrow after work?" he asked.

Stunned by his sudden change of subject, Pepper shrugged. "I'm not sure. Why?"

A mischievous grin spread across his face. "I have something for you."

Pepper patted the horse's nose once more before fully turning to face Nolan. "I'm afraid to ask."

He reached out and brushed her hair off her shoulder. With a featherlight touch, he trailed his fingertips along her jawline.

"You don't have to be afraid, Pepper. Never of me."

His voice held such conviction, and she wanted to believe him. But she knew all too well that there was no way to avoid heartache…and Nolan's name was written all over it.

Eleven

For the first time since Pepper opened her shop, she was anxious for the final customer to leave. But this particular older lady was becoming a regular. She had discovered the woman was a widow of five years and had a fondness for fresh flowers in nearly every room of her home. Pepper was all too willing to feed her addiction.

She purchased three arrangements and one of the larger paintings and, thankfully, stayed only ten minutes past her regular closing time. With a sale like that, Pepper would gladly work overtime. She'd just turned the closed sign around and flicked the lock on the old glass door when the shop cell phone rang.

Figuring it was someone asking the hours, which

was the most common phone call, Pepper crossed the shop and reached over the counter for the phone.

"Painted Pansies."

"Pepper, this is—"

"Mrs. Wright," Pepper stated. Her heart kicked up as she rubbed her abdomen and prayed for strength. "You're supposed to go through my attorney if you need anything."

"I know that, but I wanted to talk to you as a mother."

Pepper gripped her phone so tight her hand started shaking. "I don't think this is a good idea—"

"You don't have to say anything," Mrs. Wright hurried on. "Just listen for a few minutes to what I have to say."

She closed her eyes and rested her elbow on the counter. Before she could reply, the older woman clearly took the silence as the green light to continue.

"I just want you to put yourself in my place," she started, her voice quivering. "I've lost my only child and there's a part of him that will live on. I want to be part of my grandchild's life. I know you don't know me, but you have to agree that my lifestyle and finances are in far better shape. Don't you want that for your child?"

It took every ounce of tact for Pepper to keep from exploding. Yes, she wanted a great life for her child, but money and a staid home life weren't it.

"From one mother to another, let me tell you this." Gathering her strength, Pepper pushed away from the counter and paced her shop. "You of all people should know what it's like to have your only child taken from you. Is that really what you want to do? This child needs his mother. I never said I would cut you out completely—you assumed and took it upon yourself to come at me. If you have anything else you need to say, call my attorney. Don't contact me again."

Pepper disconnected the call and held the cell phone to her side. Her whole body trembled and she had no clue how she was going to make it through this custody case. Her sanity could handle only so much and she truly needed to remain stress-free.

After taking several deep breaths and counting backward from fifty, Pepper had reined in her anger and fear…somewhat.

She went to the back and pulled a large painting from her overstock. She needed to straighten up the shop just a bit before leaving. With so many sales today, she had several holes in her displays. Restocking nightly was a wonderful problem to have and it kept her busy. For a few minutes at least, she could keep her mind on doing what she loved.

Nolan had mentioned a surprise for her and between the phone call and gearing up to face him, she needed to do something that was just for her. She was so thankful for this shop, for the talents she possessed that gave her the ability to make a living out of her passions.

It wasn't that long ago that the idea of settling down would have made her twitchy, but now she was thrilled. When she'd left before, she'd been nervous, scared. Then she'd gone and traveled so much and felt so free she hadn't given settling down another thought.

Now that she was back, though, she knew this was the perfect place to set down roots. She wanted her baby to experience the beautiful small town with a large-city feel. The farms, the parks, the amazing school. Everything Pepper had ever loved was right here in Stone River.

Everything and everyone.

She finished the displays and realized she couldn't put off meeting Nolan any longer. She had no idea the surprise he had in store, but if it involved his talented lips or roaming hands, she wasn't sure she had the willpower to keep telling her husband no.

When the back door opened and clicked shut, Pepper pivoted toward the rear of the store. Who was coming in the back door, which she had locked? The contractor had already left for the day.

Nolan stepped through the opening as if he owned the place—but a man like that dominated anywhere he went. Her heart was no different.

"Did you just get out of work?" she asked.

He continued to stalk toward her with that devilish gleam in his eyes. "I didn't work today. I'm actually off for several days."

Pepper tipped her head to the side and crossed her arms. "Something you failed to mention."

With a careless shrug, he flashed that killer smile. "I was busy doing other things."

"Like trying to get my clothes off?"

His eyes raked over her from head to toe and back

up. "When I want your clothes off, darlin', they'll be off. But I didn't want you to get stressed about me being home. I actually took the time off since Hayes is coming in soon. Plus, I thought I could help you."

Pepper narrowed her gaze. "With what?"

"Nothing as naughty as what you're thinking," he assured her with a low, masculine laugh. "I'm taking you to pick out baby things."

"Baby things?"

"Furniture, bedding, clothes. Whatever you want for the baby. Everything, actually, since I'm guessing you haven't bought anything."

Stunned, Pepper blinked, trying to imagine the cost this would be. "No, you don't have to do that."

"You're right, I don't. But I'm going to and you can either come with me and pick out what you want or take the chance with me getting things on my own. I admit I don't know one stroller from the next."

She stared at him, realizing he was completely serious. Emotions overwhelmed her, as the burning in her throat was a telltale sign that she was about to lose it.

"Oh, no." He reached into his pocket and produced a handkerchief. "No tears."

What man carried around a handkerchief? Why did he have to be so incredible when she desperately needed him to be a troll? If he were a troll or a conceited jerk, it would be so much easier to leave him in the end.

But as things stood now, she was sinking further and further into the perfect role of Nolan Elliott's wife…and she loved playing that role. It was what she'd always wanted.

Pepper took the cloth and hiccupped. "Since when do you carry these?"

"Since you started crying."

She dabbed her eyes. "Damn you for making me want to be selfish and take you up on your offer."

"It's not selfish," he corrected, taking the handkerchief from her and gently swiping her cheeks. "You're going to be a wonderful mother. I'm just helping to make the transition easier."

"I don't want you doing this out of guilt."

Nolan dropped his hand and closed the space between them. "I'm doing this because I care for you, Pepper, and I want to give you something to be happy about. For a few hours we're going to forget the case, the renovations and the fact you want me as much as I want you and are fighting it every step of the way."

Pepper opened her mouth to argue, but he put his finger over her parted lips.

"Let's not waste time denying the truth."

She shoved his hand away. "I'm not denying anything, but I should tell you that Mrs. Wright called me earlier. We need to let your attorney know."

Nolan's face hardened, the muscles in his jaw tensing. "What did she want?"

"To talk to me, mother to mother." Pepper shook her head and released a sigh. "I'll tell you about it later. I want go look at baby things and forget everything else like you suggested. I need some retail therapy in the worst way."

"At the expense of my credit card?" he asked, raising his dark brows.

"Hey, you offered. There's no woman that would turn down a shopping spree on someone else's dime."

With a bark of laughter, Nolan wrapped an arm around her shoulders and started heading toward the back exit.

She stopped just before they reached the door. "Thank you, though. Seriously. I don't know what I'd do without you."

"I have faith in you, Pepper. You would've gotten through this just fine. But as long as I'm around, you won't have to do it alone."

She knew all of that but worried for the day when he wouldn't be around. Because their time together was slowly ticking to a close and eventually he would move on...just like last time. Despite the close bond they were forging now, the end was inevitable and she needed to remind herself of that in an attempt to avoid getting hurt...if such a thing was even possible.

Nolan stared at what used to be his spacious living room. Now the open space was adorned with bags and boxes, a high chair, some portable sleeper he forgot the name of, and piles and piles of clothes. There was also a plethora of rattles, teethers and bibs.

He'd honestly had no idea what he'd been in for when he suggested going shopping. He figured a crib, some diapers, a stroller, and they'd be outta there. After all, how much stuff did one tiny being need?

Pepper's hands covered her belly as she surveyed

all the paraphernalia. Then those gray eyes turned to him and the widest smile spread across her face. And that was when he realized he'd spend three times this amount to see that light back in her eyes. She'd been like a whirlwind going from aisle to aisle in every store he took her to. She'd had the sales clerks fawning all over her.

"Did we go overboard?" she asked innocently.

"Not if you're having quintuplets."

Her nose scrunched as she glanced around the room again. "I did kind of go crazy, didn't I?"

Considering they still had custom-ordered furniture to be delivered in a few weeks, maybe. But he didn't care. Once she'd started, she'd gotten on a roll and he wasn't about to stop her.

"Nothing wrong with being excited. You should see Annabelle and Colt with the twins. Colt is over the moon for those girls. He bought them matching cowgirl boots and hats. They can't even walk yet."

Pepper's eyes went big. "Cowboy boots. Why didn't I think of that?"

"There's still plenty of time," he laughed.

"What if he's not with me when it's time to buy his first pair?" she whispered in a stricken tone.

Heaviness settled in his chest. He'd bargain with the devil himself to make sure she kept her child. He was already working on plan B, but he hoped the Wrights came to their senses before he had to resort to desperate measures.

Nolan crossed to her and pulled her against his

chest. "You will be with your son for all of his firsts. You can't keep letting doubt steal your happiness."

Pepper clutched at his shirt and sniffed. He knew this wasn't all pregnancy hormones. She was legitimately afraid of what the future held.

"Do you trust me?"

When she didn't answer, Nolan eased back and tipped her chin up with his thumb. Misty eyes met his and another punch of guilt hit him in the gut. Of course she didn't trust him. He was still trying to prove to her that he wasn't the man he used to be.

"I won't let them take your son," he vowed. "I know we haven't exactly tackled the past, but you have to believe I will make this right."

Pepper blinked away the tears and attempted a smile. "I believe you'll try, but even you can't play God, Nolan. No matter how much money and resources you have. Ultimately, this will come down to the opinion of a judge. The picture the Wrights are painting of me isn't a flattering one and on paper they are a better choice."

"Like hell they are." He framed her face between his hands to make sure she kept her focus on him. "You can take some time to feel sorry for yourself, but then we're moving on. We're staying positive and we're going to fight this battle together. I married you so you'd keep your son."

Damn it. He cared for her, didn't she see that? After all these years, all this heartache and elapsed time, he cared too damn much and it was tearing him apart.

"I have just as much at stake here, too," he went on, unable to keep his mouth shut. He'd curse himself later for exposing his vulnerable side. "I'm opening myself to the past, seeing you pregnant again, part of me wishing that child was mine."

Pepper's mouth dropped as she continued to stare up at him in disbelief. "You don't mean that," she murmured.

"I don't say anything I don't mean. I want you, Pepper. I want you with a fierceness that didn't exist before. I want you to trust me with everything…and that includes your body. I want more than you just taking my name. I want you in my bed."

He didn't give her a chance to answer. Nolan slammed his mouth over hers, wrapping his arms around her waist to secure her perfectly against his body. He'd think about the consequences later. For now, however, he wanted her with a fiery passion that nearly consumed him. If only he could convince her to let that blasted guard down and allow him in.

Pepper hesitated for all of two seconds, the longest of his life, before she threw her arms around his shoulders and threaded her fingers through his hair.

Nolan scooped her up and carried her to the large leather sectional. Without looking, he swiped a hand over the packages, sending them clattering to the hardwood floors.

"Nolan," she panted against his mouth.

"Don't stop me," he all but begged. Wait, he didn't beg. He'd *never* begged. But he was damn well going to if she put the brakes on.

"I need you," she whispered.

He gazed into her eyes, saw that desire he'd been feeling staring right back at him. Those three words were the sweetest he'd ever heard.

"You'll have me," he promised.

Twelve

Pepper didn't care about all the reasons she shouldn't do this. She didn't care that they were about to consummate the hell out of this marriage. Nolan's lips and hands continued to torment her in the most delicious ways. Everything about this moment was so familiar yet so new. They were different people now but so very much reminiscent of the young lovers they'd once been.

In a flurry of hands and clothes, Pepper found herself beneath Nolan. Her bare back against the leather, his weight settled between her thighs. He brushed her hair away from her face, dropping heated kisses along her jawline.

Pepper arched her back, needing more, aching for a touch and a passion only this man could provide. Her husband. She was about to make love to her *husband*.

"I don't have protection," she confessed, hating to discuss this in the midst of things, but it was necessary.

Resting his weight on his forearms alongside her head, he met her gaze. "I'm clean, Pepper. You're the only other woman I've not been careful with and I have regular blood work."

"I'm clean, too."

She wasn't about to get into how she became pregnant because of a condom malfunction. Now wasn't the time to bring that story to light.

Pepper wrapped her legs around Nolan's waist, locking her knees behind his back. The silent plea for him to join their bodies worked like a charm. Nolan slid into her and everything else ceased to exist. *Finally.* That was the only thought that entered her mind. She was finally back where she belonged.

Nolan shifted his weight and stilled. "Am I hurting you, darlin'?"

"No." She trailed her fingertips over his taut, muscular back. "You're perfect."

And he was. Perfect now, perfect in her life, perfect as her husband. But she refused to delve into the fact that this was all temporary. She was holding on to this moment, this man.

Nolan's weight pressing her into the sofa was absolutely glorious. His strength, his determination to make her his top priority, was even more arousing than nearly anything else. He cared for her, whether he wanted to admit how deeply or not. The way he touched her with such exquisite tenderness, the way he moved with her, caressing her and raining kisses all over her face and neck…it was abundantly clear that his feelings went far beyond just that of a physical relationship and marriage of convenience. This entire ordeal was anything but convenient.

Nolan's warm breath tickled the side of her neck as he rested his forehead against hers. Pepper was barely holding on—she didn't want this to end, didn't want to face the other side of their intimacy. But her body had other ideas. The faster he moved, the more Pepper lost control, until she finally could hold out no longer.

Her entire body tightened as she clutched his shoulders. He whispered something in her ear, but she couldn't make it out. Every part of her trembled and before she could come down from her high, Nolan followed. He arched back, the muscles in his neck straining, his shoulders tense as he tried to keep his weight off her. Even now, she was his number one thought.

Pepper stroked her hands up and down his back as his breathing started to slow back to normal. When he eased up, she pressed her palms flat against him.

"Stay here. You're not hurting me and this feels too good."

Once he got up, they'd have to talk or wallow in awkward silence. But she wasn't ready for either option at the moment.

"If I'd known shopping for baby things was all it took to get you naked, I would've done this on day one."

Pepper laughed. So much for the awkward silence. "That's not why we ended up here. I'd say it was inevitable, even though that annulment is going to be impossible now."

He lifted his head and flashed that killer smile. "Baby, I could've told you that. There's no way I can be with you again, especially in my house, and not have you."

"This could complicate things."

"It could if we let it." He shifted once again, somehow flipping them to where she straddled his lap and she found herself looking down into his deep blue eyes. "We're adults, we're married, we know this is temporary. Why can't we just enjoy each other for as long as it lasts?"

He made the situation sound so simple. But her heart was already tumbling and she had no doubt that she was going to leave at the end of this ordeal with a heartache. Would the pain compare to the last time? She had no clue, but she truly didn't want to be so broken. It had taken her literally years to recover.

"Don't worry about tomorrow," he told her quietly. His hands settled over her belly. "This little guy is all that matters and I'm here to make sure you both get what you deserve. And that's a lifetime of happiness."

A lifetime without Nolan in her life. Once he saw that she was secure, he'd move on. He'd go back to being married to his work. He'd made no promises beyond helping her keep her baby and she should be grateful. She *was* grateful, but she was also greedy. Now that she'd slept with him, she feared walking away wouldn't be an option, and Nolan wasn't about to make this marriage permanent.

Which brought her right back around to that heartache she didn't want. A little too late to be having regrets, she reminded herself. She needed this marriage, needed Nolan, and her feelings didn't matter in the long run.

When he slid his hands up her abdomen and over her breasts, Pepper let the worries go for now. It was getting late and her husband clearly had other plans…

The pounding on the door jolted Nolan from sleep. In a tangle of arms and legs, he quickly realized he and Pepper hadn't moved from the couch. Apparently they'd worn each other out.

With a quick glance, he saw that his wife was still asleep. Her dark lashes lay against her creamy skin, her slightly parted mouth sorely tempting him to ignore the knocking and remain right where he was… taking full advantage of those lush lips.

Pepper stirred, and Nolan quickly untangled himself. He wanted to get to the door before the uninvited visitor woke her.

Scanning the room, he finally spotted his boxer briefs and jeans. He danced from one leg to the other down the hallway, and he'd just gotten the jeans zipped when he reached the door. He quickly flipped the lock and jerked the door open.

"Oh." Annabelle jumped back, a hand over her heart. "I thought you were home, but…"

She raked her eyes over him. "I'm so sorry. I didn't realize you'd still be in bed."

Nolan propped his forearm on the edge of the door. "It's okay. Late night."

"Winnie made extra rolls and a casserole for you."

It was then he noticed the large basket in her hand. Damn it. He didn't want to be rude, but he also didn't want her coming in and risking seeing Pepper wearing nothing but bedhead and whisker burn.

"I can take it." He reached for the basket, but she eased it to the side and raised her brows.

"You don't want to introduce me to your wife? We're sisters-in-law, so I really should get to know her."

Nolan combed a hand through his hair and groaned. "She's—"

"Right here."

He cringed at the sound of Pepper's sexy, sleep-roughened voice behind him. Risking a glance over his shoulder, he got an eyeful of her. Even with her hair in disarray, her face void of any makeup, and her curvy body wrapped in the gray throw he kept on the sofa, Pepper was truly the most beautiful woman he'd ever seen.

"I'm so sorry." Annabelle stepped over the threshold, forcing Nolan to move back. "I just assumed Nolan would be at work and I'd get to sneak a visit with you privately."

Nolan closed the door behind her—apparently they were getting company whether he wanted it or not. He loved Annabelle like a sister, but he wasn't quite ready to share Pepper with anyone just yet.

"So you thought you'd come quiz my wife and

get in some girl talk?" Nolan asked, reaching to take the basket.

Annabelle flashed him a sheepish smile. "Maybe."

"Well, let me throw some clothes on," Pepper said. "We can kick Nolan out and get that talk in. I'm so excited to meet you. Mostly I'm excited to have another female around."

Annabelle sent him a wink as she strode on into the house. Fantastic. Despite being a man who didn't want to get sucked too far into this family lifestyle, he'd slept with his wife, forging an even deeper bond, and now his soon-to-be sister-in-law was fostering her own special connection with Pepper. And that bond would be worse because women stuck together. So if he did anything wrong or hurt Pepper in any way, Annabelle would naturally side with Pepper. Then she would tell Colt, and Nolan would have to hear about it from his baby brother.

The inevitable snowball effect already gave him a migraine.

One thing was for sure, Nolan didn't want to stay around for this little meeting. He had a few days off and he intended to get back to his roots and enjoy some old-fashioned manual labor. No doubt Colt would appreciate the extra hands.

Besides, this would give him some space to figure out where to go from here. Turned out he wasn't done with Pepper. Not by a long shot. They'd consummated their marriage, but he wanted more. More of Pepper in his life…and in his bed. This marriage might be in name only for the sake of her unborn child, but as long as they were man and wife, he fully intended to use that to his advantage. He doubted he'd get too many complaints from Pepper if that satisfied smile on her face this morning was any indicator.

He couldn't wait to get back and have her all to himself again.

Thirteen

"I should apologize about barging in, but I've been dying to meet you."

Pepper laughed, appreciating the woman's candor. "These cinnamon rolls smell delicious."

"Yeah, Winnie is a master in the kitchen."

Pepper sat down across from Annabelle. Once Nolan had left—more like made tracks getting out of his house—Pepper had led Annabelle out into the enclosed patio room. The mouthwatering aroma of the fresh pastries had reminded Pepper just how hungry she truly was. Last night had…well, it had been nothing short of amazing and magical and all of those euphoric adjectives that came to mind when describing the best sexual experience of her life.

"And she didn't want to bring these and check me out herself?"

Annabelle laughed as she tore apart a gooey roll. "She said she remembers you from when you and Nolan were together before. She said she always liked you and I could take a turn coming. But be warned. She's preparing more food for tomorrow and will be here to pay you a visit."

"I'll be fat by the time this marriage is over." She smoothed a hand down her swollen midsection. "Well, fatter."

"You're stunning." Annabelle's brows rose as she twisted the diamond engagement ring on her finger. "So you're only married for the baby?"

Why lie? It wasn't like they had to pretend to be in love. Love didn't exist, not for them, anyway. No matter how much Pepper felt for Nolan, she knew better than to hope for a happily-ever-after with him. She was a grown woman, a realistic woman, and had her eyes wide-open.

"I just want to keep custody," she explained, pulling apart her roll. "The father of my baby passed away, something I didn't know until recently, because we had parted ways before I even found out I was expecting. He paid me a lump sum of money as his way of support and wanted to be left out of the upbringing."

"Sounds like a jerk," Annabelle muttered. "Sorry. Go on."

Pepper put a bite in her mouth and nearly moaned

as the flavors exploded on her tongue. This might be the best thing she'd ever tasted.

"They're amazing, right?" Annabelle said around her own bite.

"I can't even find words," Pepper groaned. "Where was I?"

"Discussing why your marriage is going to end."

Pepper took a sip of her juice and ripped off another bite. "Nolan and I have a history. I don't know what all Colt has told you."

"He pretty much gave me all the details of the past."

That made this conversation a bit easier. "Then that brings you up to speed on why this is so awkward for us now. I mean, those old feelings are there, but then there's so much going on and we definitely aren't the same people we used to be."

Annabelle reached across the table and patted Pepper's hand. "Honey, life knocks us all down, but it's those feelings deep down, those that you can't ignore, that pull you through."

Pepper drew in a shaky breath. She didn't want to count on those feelings that lived deep inside her. Those were the ones that scared her, the ones that kept her up at night and made her wonder.

"Well, I've got so much going on right now I can't even think about my feelings for Nolan."

"You love him." Annabelle's matter-of-fact tone had Pepper stilling. "I saw it in the way you looked at him. He loves you, too, or you wouldn't be here."

"Oh, I'm not so sure about that," Pepper laughed,

trying to lighten the intense mood. "He's a player. That much I know for sure."

"Maybe so, but he's never brought another woman here. Colt said he's been very adamant about that. He thinks of this place as some type of sanctuary, some-place he can escape everything and be alone. His job is demanding and so is the ranch."

Pepper waved a hand in the air before diving back into her roll. "He married me to help me out of a bind...that's all. It would've looked rather silly for us to live separately. Besides, my apartment had a slight fire. It's getting renovated now."

Annabelle quirked a brow and smiled. "But he didn't have to do anything, did he? He could've let you deal with everything on your own."

No, no, he didn't have to step in, but guilt often made people do things they otherwise wouldn't. Pep-per wasn't going to keep defending her position, be-cause she was exhausted and Annabelle clearly had stars in her eyes. Of course she was happy, engaged to an Elliott brother and raising twin babies. Her whole world was perfectly in place. Pepper wanted to visit there for just a bit. What she wouldn't give to have just one day of pure bliss and no worries...

"Let's not talk about my crazy life," Pepper said. "I want to hear about your girls. Nolan said you have twin girls. I bet you're tired."

Annabelle laughed. "It's challenging, for sure. But they're so sweet and fun."

"I'd love to meet them."

"Of course." Annabelle took a drink of her juice,

holding on to her cup as she swirled the liquid. "They're with my dad right now. I didn't know if I should bombard you with my zoo for our first meeting. I didn't want to scare you in case I liked you and wanted to be friends."

With a laugh, Pepper leaned back in her seat and shook her head. "Please. I'd love to be bombarded by babies. I have no idea what to expect and I'm terrified."

"That's understandable," the other woman told her with a sympathetic smile. "Why don't you come down to the main house and you can meet them? Unless you have something else you're doing this morning."

Pepper smiled, feeling like she was making a new friend, and one she desperately needed. A female ally could quite possibly be the outlet she needed to get through.

Because in a few hours, Nolan would be back and they'd have to talk about last night. She wanted to know where they'd go from here. She didn't want to play that female card and ask for a label on their relationship—this complicated mess was too chaotic to try to define. But she did feel that she deserved to know what he was thinking and feeling.

And she'd be sure to guard her own emotions until she knew. Getting a broken heart from Nolan Elliott once in her life was all she could handle.

"If you slam one more thing, I'm going to make you leave."

Nolan gripped the brush, ready to fling it back

into the bucket, but caught himself. He'd been in a pissy mood since leaving his house. Probably right about now, he figured, the women were knee-deep in gossip, and he'd wager a bet that every topic had his name on it.

He scowled, wishing Annabelle had never shown up at his door with those damn cinnamon rolls. The last thing he'd wanted was to leave Pepper after their incredible night together. He'd wanted to stay, to take her upstairs, and do it all over again. But would she welcome this new twist in their relationship? Or would she put the brakes on because she didn't want to get too attached? He knew Pepper well enough to know she led with her heart.

When he'd first left, he'd been in a great mood, thinking of last night and how happy Pepper had seemed. But then reality settled deep and now that devil on his shoulder was putting negative thoughts in his head.

He thought he'd grown since they'd been together last. He'd believed he could sleep with Pepper without getting more involved. But he'd been a fool. The daydreams he had about her, about this marriage, were all too real...and all too consuming.

Damn it. He didn't want to hurt her, but he wasn't about to turn back. He wanted his wife in the most basic, primal way a man wanted a woman. And now that he'd had her again, all that passion they'd shared before came rushing back and he refused to let it go after he'd had a taste.

"Bad night?" Colt asked, stepping into the doorway of the stall. "Or are you mad because Annabelle interrupted something?"

Nolan grunted. "Shut up."

"You're the one who got yourself into this mess. Don't get grouchy with me."

Nolan tossed the brush into the bucket anyway. "You think I don't know how I got into this? I had little choice, though."

Colt hooked his thumbs in his belt and shook his head. "You don't believe that any more than I do."

Nolan didn't know what to believe. Right now he was too keyed up about last night to worry about too much more. Having Pepper back in his bed, so to speak, was all he'd wanted, a temptation he couldn't resist. But now that he'd had her, he wasn't so sure he wanted her to be anywhere else. Of course, then there was the whole issue that he didn't want to be married with a family, yet here he was. He'd *volunteered* to put himself in that exact position.

Nolan patted Doc's side. He needed a good ride, but he'd groomed his stallion instead. Doc needed some downtime today.

"All I know is she's turning me inside out, but then I think, this is not my cross to bear."

"Are you sure about that? Sounds like years of guilt have caught up with you."

Nolan blew out a breath and turned to face his baby brother. "I can't turn back the clock. I'm not the same young jerk I was, but I'm honest about what I can give. She knows I'm still not wanting a family. We're taking it day by day, I guess."

Colt merely raised his brows but Nolan didn't care what his brother thought, or anyone else, for that matter. He had enough of his own turmoil to deal with.

"You're playing house with a woman you were once in love with who's pregnant and back in town for good, and you think you can be this calm about it?" Colt snorted and tipped his hat back on his head. "I'll play along with your delusions if you want. Besides, I'll get all the details from Annabelle when she comes home later."

Growling, Nolan pushed passed his brother. He headed down the stone walkway between the stalls and ignored Colt's obnoxious laughter. Surely Pepper wouldn't spill everything. Of course, there was no hiding the fact Annabelle had gotten them out of bed, or off the couch, as the case may be. That would be enough fuel for Colt to assume that Nolan was falling into this whole married-bliss phase.

Nolan refused to let that happen. Yes, he might want to be physical with Pepper, he might be doing all of this to help her, and fine, he might be a tad jealous that she carried another man's baby, but he didn't want to settle down for real. Wasn't his life busy enough? He was perfectly fulfilled without adding more. Being a doctor and a rancher was full-time. Adding a child into the mix would only spread him even thinner and that wouldn't be fair to an innocent baby.

"You still picking Hayes up from the airport?" Nolan asked as he grabbed a blanket. He planned on taking out Lightning, Colt's stallion.

"That's my horse," Colt stated. "Use your own."

"Mine needs to rest and you haven't taken Lightning out yet." Nolan ignored his brother's protest. "I need to get away and think. I'll do a perimeter check of the fence line."

"Running from your problems didn't work so well the first time you were with Pepper. What makes you think it will this time?"

Nolan tossed the blanket over Lightning's back and smoothed it out. "I didn't come down here to ask your opinion. I came to work, to ride and to give the women time to talk about us and do their nails...or whatever the hell else they're doing."

Colt laughed. Bastard. Nolan wasn't in the mood for jokes or laughter. He wanted to wallow in his dark mood because the more he thought about last night, the more he was conflicted. He wanted to go back to the house and take Pepper to his bed and forget the world existed.

Nolan fixed the saddle in place and threw a glance toward Colt. "I'll bring him back in a few hours."

"Why don't you let me and my guys do the work and you go back home to Pepper?"

Nolan led Lightning outside. Colt followed behind. "Why don't you focus on your own woman and leave mine to me."

He mounted the stallion and kicked him into a gallop. Nolan could get work done and hopefully clear his head. By the time he got back home, maybe he'd have all the answers. Most likely he'd still be confused, but he was sure of one thing...he'd still want

Pepper in his bed. That would never change. It was just what they would do outside the bedroom that he had to worry about.

Fourteen

Nolan slid his cell back into his pocket and breathed a sigh of relief. Well, somewhat. His PI had dug through the Wrights' dirty laundry and discovered something useful. If that family was going to fight, he was damn well going to come back at them full force.

He couldn't wait to tell Pepper. She needed something positive to focus on right now and discussing the case, in a positive way, would hopefully alleviate some of the awkwardness that would surely surround them as soon as he stepped inside and they were alone once again.

He'd been gone over three hours and had no more answers now than he had when he set out to check the fence lines. He needed a shower, he could use a drink, and he wanted his wife. If he could multitask and have all three at the same time, well, he'd call this day one of the best in a long time.

The shrieking alarm echoing through the open patio doors had Nolan charging inside, the fantasy ripped away. Why the hell was his smoke alarm going off? Where was Pepper? Was she okay?

As soon as he stepped into the kitchen, he quickly realized she was indeed okay…but their dinner wasn't. Pepper had a towel and was smacking the hell out of a casserole dish on top of the stove. Nolan couldn't help the laugh that escaped him.

Pepper spun around, met his gaze, then saw that her towel was on fire, so she beat the casserole once again. With a sigh and a muttered curse, she tossed the towel into the sink in the center island and doused it with water. When she leaned her hands on the smooth granite countertop, Nolan crossed the room.

"There's always takeout."

Pepper narrowed her eyes. "If you tell Winnie that I burnt her casserole, I will tell her about the time you used her favorite pan to make me dinner and ruined it because you burnt the bottom and she never could figure out who did it."

Nolan mimicked her actions and rested his palms on the island opposite her. "She'll never hear it from me. But tell me, was it the chicken-and-broccoli casserole? Because that's my favorite and I'd hate to cry in front of you."

"Actually, it was. I guess I owe you one." Pepper wrinkled her nose. "I'm really sorry. I wanted to have a late lunch all planned and I wasn't sure when you'd be back. I was getting hungry and I figured I'd heat this up, but then I called the doctor and got sidetracked—"

"What doctor? Why?" Immediately, he came around the side of the island and gripped her shoulders, turning her to face him. "What's wrong?"

"I just had some minor bleeding, but I wasn't cramping or anything and it stopped almost as fast as it started. I just wanted them to know."

"I'm your first call if something is wrong," he commanded. "I could've taken you to the hospital to get checked out. Matter of fact, let's go. We'll get an ultrasound and listen for the baby's heartbeat and—"

"I'm fine," she assured him. "I've felt the baby move and my doctor promised that this was normal and most likely from intercourse. Every pregnancy is different, so there's no textbook case. He said as long as I feel fine and I still feel the baby, there's nothing to be alarmed about."

But there was everything to be alarmed about. When she'd miscarried before, she'd felt fine. Everything had been going great with the pregnancy, their child had been healthy...and then suddenly out of the blue she was gone.

The fear of years ago slithered through him, squeezing like a vise around his chest.

"Go up and lie down. I'll make something and bring it to you."

Pepper tipped her head to the side. "I'm perfectly fine. I know what my body needs and right now it's just food. I've been sitting all day talking with Annabelle. I went down to their house and met the twins. They are absolutely adorable, by the way."

Nolan slid his hands down her arms, feathering his touch until he stepped back for distance. "You probably overdid it, then. Those girls are a handful."

Pepper smiled and patted his cheek. "They're twins under a year old. Of course they're a handful. That's pretty much their only job right now."

"Still, you don't need to be doing too much."

Pepper glanced to the stove, where the dish was still smoking. "Apparently, I can't do anything. I could probably whip up a grilled cheese. I'd say that's safe."

Nolan pulled his hat off and swiped his forehead with the back of his arm. "I need a shower in the worst way. I was going to have you join me, but I don't think that's a good idea with hemorrhaging."

Those bright eyes widened. "Nolan, I'm not here to scratch your itch or be at your command. Yes, I want you and I'm not sorry for last night, but I also can't pretend this is real."

Well, the way she said it made him sound foolish.

"I won't apologize for wanting you, Pepper." And he wouldn't look coldhearted, either. "Our feelings are mutual and you can't deny that you want more. We may be a paper marriage only, but there's no reason to play the game and dance around the sexual attraction. We already proved that doesn't work."

"Maybe you're out of my system now."

When she cocked her hip and quirked her brow, Nolan took that challenge and opted to call her on it. He snaked his arms around her waist and pulled her flush against his body. Torso to torso, pelvis to pelvis. Her eyes widened with surprise. Then they betrayed her as they darted to his mouth.

"You were saying?" he murmured as he leaned in to slide his lips over hers.

"You're going to at least rest on the couch," he told her, his lips hovering over hers. "I'm going to work on dinner and grab a quick shower. You're not to move a muscle. For the rest of the day, I'll be doing everything for you."

She let out a slight whimper, one he knew she meant to hold in. He couldn't help but smile. The amount of willpower she had was no match for him. He'd bust down every barrier she tried to put up, because his need for her wasn't even close to being sated. Last night only served as a reminder of all he'd missed with her and all he wanted to explore again and again.

"I don't need to be pampered," she muttered.

Nolan gripped her backside. "Maybe it's time I showed you that's exactly what you deserve."

"You're going to make me want." She closed her eyes and rested her forehead against his. "I can't, Nolan. I can't want you."

"Keep telling yourself that."

He covered her mouth with his, and she melted against him. He didn't need to use words to prove her wrong. She couldn't deny the pull between them any more than he could. Their physical attraction had never faded, even with the gap of time they'd lost.

Nolan ended the kiss as abruptly as he'd started

it, pleased when Pepper leaned forward and had to stop herself.

"I'll get that shower and have lunch for you in no time, babe."

He turned and headed out of the room, but not before he heard her mutter, "I'm not your babe."

That stopped him. Something snapped inside him. After what they'd been through, all of it up to this point, she was his and damn it, he was going to prove to her that she couldn't lie—not to herself, not to him.

Nolan turned back around, crossed the space and enveloped her in his arms. He claimed her mouth as he arched her backward, completely consuming her. He craved this woman like nothing else and the way she gripped his biceps, moaning as his lips crushed hers, only proved she wanted this, too.

He slid his mouth along her jawline, down her throat. Pushing the strap of her tank and bra aside, he continued to trail his mouth along her heated skin. Pepper's fingertips glided through his hair as she panted his name.

"Never say you're not mine again," he growled against her lips as he released her breast.

"Nolan…"

That's right. His name would be the only one on her lips. He might not be able to make love to her now because of her tender state, but he could damn well stake his claim and have her coming apart in his arms.

He yanked her skirt to the ground to puddle at her feet. Then, stepping back, he took in the sight of her hair in disarray, her tank half hanging on her body and her standing before him in only her panties. The round belly had him reaching out, placing his palms possessively on her as he met her gaze.

Pepper's breath came out fast, her lips wet and swollen from the proof of his desire.

He fisted a handful of her hair and guided her head to the side as he went back in for another taste. Easing his fingertips along the edge of her panties, he nearly lost it when she moaned and widened her stance.

Nolan rubbed her, teasing her mercilessly, and had her jerking her hips against him. In no time she went over the brink, tearing her mouth from his as he watched her squeeze her eyes shut and cry out in pleasure.

This was the most erotic sight he'd ever seen and he damn well wasn't ready to give it up anytime soon. As long as Pepper lived in his house, legally carried his name, she was his.

"Of course. I'll be right there."

Nolan hung up his phone and shoved it back in the pocket of his jeans. Pepper had just finished her grilled chicken and salad. She wiped her mouth with her napkin and sat up in her seat.

Their intense make-out session nearly an hour ago had left both of them ravenous. He'd wanted nothing more than to take her upstairs and lay her out on his bed and finish what they'd started. But he worried it might be too much. Soon, though. He just wanted to follow up with the doctor himself and hear that she was okay.

"What's wrong?" she asked.

Nolan grabbed his keys off the counter and headed toward the garage door off the kitchen. "It's my dad. He fell and the nurse thought I'd want to come assess him before they decided what to do."

Pepper knew his father lived in an assisted-living facility. She came to her feet. "I'll go with you."

"Stay here. Dealing with my father isn't part of our agreement."

Pepper reeled back as if he'd slapped her. "You're right. It's not, but I thought…forget it. Go on."

Nolan took a step toward her. "Pepper—"

"No." She held her hands out. "You're right. This isn't a real marriage and I'm not part of your life like I used to be."

Emotions threatened to consume her, so she spun around and headed for the living room. She didn't want to see Nolan's look of regret, because she was coming to realize the only thing he regretted was the fact he was stuck with her…or at least that was how it felt.

"Come with me."

Pepper froze in the wide doorway. Nolan's boots shuffled against the hardwood as he moved in behind her. She took a deep breath.

"Just go, Nolan. This is ridiculous to argue about. I'm going to go into the shop and paint. I also want to see how the renovations are coming." Ready to face him, she shifted around. "We don't have to do things together—your family isn't actually mine, I know. I don't need the reminder."

Nolan shoved a hand through his hair, still damp from the shower. "I have to go. I want you with me."

Pepper forced a smile. "No, you don't. Your first instinct was to close me out. There's no need to apologize for being who you are."

Now Pepper did leave the kitchen and went to compose herself in the privacy of her own room. She'd change her clothes and go into the shop. The sooner her apartment was ready, the sooner she would be that much closer to getting back to the life she'd planned. All she needed was her baby…not the reminder that she and Nolan were only pretending to be a fairy-tale couple.

Pepper walked through her apartment, admiring the new touches that were being added as well as how everything was blending with the old charm of the building. The kitchen had custom white cabinets now as opposed to the old dated oak. The backsplash looked like something out of a magazine. She leaned over the open cabinet. She had no idea what the countertop would look like once installed, but as she ran her fingertip over the backsplash, she marveled at the smooth glass finish in a pale blue.

If the half-done kitchen was looking this modern yet cozy and chic, she couldn't wait to see the final product. She'd definitely have to paint some new pieces to be added into her new space.

Careful to step over tools and materials, Pepper made her way down the hall. The room she planned on using for the nursery had the door closed. The last time she'd stopped in, it had been open, and she'd gone in and done a little fantasy decorating.

Pepper eased the door open and stood in shock as she took in the sight of a nearly finished nursery. The far wall with two windows had been painted navy. A silhouette of a horse with two colts was painted in a pale gray between the two windows. The other three walls were the same pale gray and had various rustic touches. There was a cluster of wood slats with horseshoes hanging at an angle as if to be used for hooks. One wall had a cowboy hat and in cursive font curving around the brim it said Future Cowboy.

Pepper noted the new hardwood floors in a dark wood that went with the male theme. Everything was perfect. She hadn't told Nolan or even the contractor she wanted this room done, and she actually wasn't a bit upset that she didn't get to paint it. This was exactly what she would've wanted for her son. Something simple yet very much part of the lifestyle that would embrace him here in Stone River, Texas.

There was no way the contractor had done all of this on his own, or even at all. And there was no doubt who was the mastermind behind this decision.

One minute he was shutting her out, the next he was going out of his way to make sure she had everything she needed. How could she keep up with her already jumbled emotions?

The shifting in her belly had her placing her hands over the movement. In a few months she could welcome her son into this room. She could already imagine a rocker in the corner where she'd cuddle him to sleep. She'd always heard about that special bond between a mother and her son, and Pepper was convinced now more than ever that they would be tight. After all, who else did they have?

They would be a team and she would protect him from all harm. And that included letting strangers raise him. Pepper would be absolutely gutted if she had to hand over her child. To lose a child in any way was something no parent should have to go through— didn't the Wrights see that?

Pepper's cell chimed from the pocket of her maxi skirt. She reached in and frowned at the display. Why would the attorney be calling on a Saturday?

This couldn't be a good sign, could it? Was something wrong? Had there been a crimp in the case?

With a shaky hand, she answered.

"Hello?"

"Pepper, I tried calling Nolan, but he didn't answer. I hope this isn't a bad time."

Of course he hadn't answered. He was with his father and he was off work for the next few days.

"No. This is fine. Is something wrong?" There seemed to be so many ups and downs lately, she didn't know how many more she could handle.

"Nolan had hired an investigator to dig into the Wrights," he stated.

Pepper gripped the phone. She'd been completely unaware of any of this. Why hadn't he told her what he'd done? How much more had that cost? She refused to be any more indebted to him than she already was, but part of her was thrilled he'd thought to have them investigated. That was brilliant, especially because she needed to know everything about the couple who could possibly take her son from her.

Still, why hadn't Nolan told her? Sure, they were married just for pretenses, but this was a big deal and he'd kept vital information from her.

"Their attorney has been notified of the findings and the Wrights want to know if you would consider settling out of court. They've offered one generous sum to compensate you."

"What the hell does that mean?" she all but yelled. "They want to buy my child? They offered money once and I don't care what they're offering now. I won't take it."

Pepper's heart kicked up as fury bubbled within her. "What were the findings from the investigator?"

"Apparently the Wrights owe quite a bit of back taxes and their financial state isn't as glossy as they like to portray."

Pepper considered exactly what this meant. "How would they pay me, then?" she asked.

"I have no clue," he replied. "But I think they're going to tell you anything to get custody at this point. They've lost their son and they desperately want to hang on to him in any way possible."

Pepper understood that need. She'd do anything to hang on to her son, as well. Hadn't she married the only man she'd ever loved? Wasn't she living in his home, playing house, just to make sure her son remained with her?

Already she was that parent who would go to any

length to make a secure, stable environment for her child. And she wasn't the least bit sorry. Her emotions, her worries about her own life, didn't matter.

"I have my store to run, so any meeting would have to be in the evening and Nolan goes back to work next week," she explained.

"I'll get it set up and let you know. We're going to win this, Pepper. It's almost over."

She could only nod as emotions threatened to overtake her. Damn pregnancy hormones.

After disconnecting the call, she gave a final once-over to the nursery. Inspiration for new paintings flooded her mind and she was eager to get downstairs. To have her own artwork in her son's room was an absolute must.

She needed to do something creative—that was the only way she'd calm her mind. Not to mention that seemed to be the only thing she could control right now. Her emotions were out of her control, this case was out of her control, and her marriage was out of her control. Coincidentally, Nolan occupied real estate in each of those areas.

She'd let his words hurt her earlier and she knew better than that. For a moment, she'd let that guard down and her heart had suffered the fallout. She wouldn't make that mistake again.

Fifteen

By the time Pepper got home, she was definitely relaxed. So much so she felt as if she could fall asleep at any minute. She'd painted three pictures, all with her son's room in mind, but she wasn't sure how she'd arrange them. Once she had the furniture placed, she'd get a better idea of how she wanted all of the wall art.

She came through the garage door that led to the kitchen. The four globe lights suspended over the massive island were on, but Nolan wasn't in here. His vehicles were here, but he could've taken the four-wheeler down to one of the stables.

Her stomach growled and she nearly groaned. The pretzels and banana she'd shoved in her purse and devoured two hours ago had already worn off. She wasn't about to attempt to make something, and most likely Nolan had already had dinner, so she figured she'd go for the mature peanut-butter-and-jelly sandwich.

Pepper slipped her sandals off by the door and dropped her bag onto the kitchen table. Her bangle bracelets jingled with each movement. She'd put on her favorite set earlier, the one with the newest charm of a silver baby rattle. It was just one of the many pieces that had been waiting for her in her new closet when she'd come to Nolan's house.

"Hey."

Nolan came through the wide doorway and strode toward her. With a smile lighting his handsome face, those well-worn jeans hugging his narrow hips and a fitted gray T-shirt showing off his muscles, he didn't look like a master surgeon...he looked like every woman's fantasy.

"How's your dad?" she asked.

"He's all right. He fell trying to get into bed and he's bruised his hip pretty good, but thankfully, nothing is broken." Nolan crossed the room, his eyes raking over her. "You look exhausted."

"Ironically, I feel exhausted." She yawned, unable to hold it back. "I'm ready for food and bed. In that order, but hopefully within the next few minutes for both."

Nolan laughed and reached out. Before she realized his intent, he'd scooped her up and cradled her against his chest. Pepper didn't have much choice, so she looped her arms around his neck.

"And what are you doing?" she asked breathlessly as he carried her out of the room.

"Apologizing for being a jerk earlier and showing you that you deserve to be pampered. I wasn't sure when you'd be home, but I knew you'd be hungry and probably tired."

When he stepped into the living room, Pepper gasped at the spread on the floor. Laid out over the dark hardwood floors was a thick blanket. Random takeout boxes were set off to one side, bottles of water and a small bouquet of wildflowers next to the boxes.

"Are you apologizing or seducing me again?" she asked coyly. Suddenly her hurt from earlier disappeared, replaced by an emotion she refused to identify because that would cross that line into opening her heart.

"Both." He looked down into her eyes, and for a moment Pepper forgot this was all a farce. "Maybe I want to seduce my wife, to show her that even though this is all temporary, I still care for her and want her to be happy."

Temporary. Yes. She'd do well to remember that.

Nolan set her on her feet. "I have a variety of tasty offerings, and I promise you won't leave here hungry."

Pepper took a seat on the blanket and crisscrossed her legs in front of her. Nolan sat across from her and opened the basket. As he pulled out dish after dish, Pepper was utterly stunned. Fruits, cheeses, crisp veggies. He even had fried chicken that instantly hit her senses and made her mouth water.

"This is Winnie's fried chicken," he explained as

he settled all the food between them. "I actually just got back from getting it. I was afraid you'd get home while I was gone."

And there went those emotions. Pepper couldn't control the tears; she didn't even try. "Damn it. Why do you do this to me?"

Nolan leaned forward and swiped her cheek with the pad of his thumb. "Because you deserve it. I keep telling you that. One day you'll listen."

Why couldn't he see what a perfect husband he'd be? Well, he was a great husband now, but for the long term, for real, Nolan would be every woman's dream.

His cell chimed and he groaned. "I'm not on call, so I know it's not the hospital. But I need to answer that because it could be about my dad."

Pepper waved her hand. "Go. I don't expect you to drop everything for me."

"Why not?" Nolan's eyes held hers as the phone continued to intrude on their moment. "You should always come first."

Pepper wasn't quite sure how to respond to that comment, so she reached for a plump strawberry. She popped it in her mouth and surveyed the rest of the spread.

"I suppose I have you to thank for the nursery in my apartment," she stated softly, ready to move on to another topic, something less to do with feelings and this new territory they'd ventured into.

Nolan nodded. "I know you'll want to decorate your way, so I told the decorator to keep it to a minimum and if you weren't pleased, she'll come back and do what you want."

"It's perfect. How did you pull all that off?"

Nolan grabbed a piece of fried chicken. "I paid her extra to come when you weren't in the shop. I didn't want you to know. Whenever you're ready, we can haul all of your baby things to the apartment and I'll help you set up his room."

Pepper's heart squeezed, but she faked a smile. "Already counting down the days until you're rid of me?"

His intense blue eyes came up to lock on to hers. "I figured you were ready for your own space and to move forward with your life when this case is over. You're more than welcome to stay here as long as you like."

He didn't mean that. Because as long as she liked would be forever, as man and wife, till death do them part.

Pepper analyzed each piece of chicken and chose the perfect one. She tore off the crispy skin and popped a bite into her mouth, nearly groaning when all those flavors hit her at once.

"You always loved Winnie's fried chicken."

Nolan was watching her, a hunger in his own eyes that was all too familiar. This *entire setup* was all too familiar.

"The first time I had her fried chicken, you set up a carpet picnic for me," she recalled. "You surprised me and I think that's when I fell in love with you."

She didn't look away; she wasn't sorry she'd told

him. He knew how she'd felt when they were together before. But this was completely different. In the time they were spending together now, they seemed to be forging a deeper bond than ever before.

"We were in love," he said gruffly, still holding her gaze. "I just…couldn't be what you wanted."

And he still couldn't. The words hung in the air between them just the same as if he'd said them aloud.

"No matter how grief stricken I was, I should've been there for you when you miscarried." He shook his head and glanced down to the blanket. "That was my child, too."

"I mourned for our baby for so long—part of me still does," she admitted.

"I mourned." His words were so low she was almost convinced she hadn't heard correctly. "After you left, I wondered what the hell I'd done. I thought of the baby that I would never see. I couldn't describe my feelings. My family was furious about how I'd treated you. It was a dark time for me."

Up until she'd lost the baby, she'd been convinced they'd marry and live happily ever after. But that was a foolish fantasy of a young, guileless girl who thought love could carry them through life.

She knew better now.

"Well, we can't go back." Pepper attempted a smile, but she hurt. Her heart literally hurt for that young couple they'd been, for the dreams she'd thought they shared but that had been only one-sided. "Thanks for everything you've done. Whether out of guilt or because you are genuinely concerned, I know this will only help my case."

Nolan leaned across the blanket. His hand gently cupped the side of her face as his lips grazed hers. Pepper closed her eyes, giving in to the moment. Letting him have his way, because she was just as eager for a taste of him.

Every time he touched her, kissed her, looked at her like he wanted to devour her, Pepper had a hard time reminding herself this was all temporary.

Sixteen

Nolan slid his fingers through Pepper's silky, dark hair. He'd always had a thing for her long hair, how it glided over his hands, over his body.

He wasn't even going to deny that he wanted her now, but he had to prove to her that even though the marriage had an expiration date, he wasn't interested in any other woman.

Pepper eased back, reaching up to grip his wrist. "I seriously need to eat. My little guy needs his nutrients."

"And you're going to need your energy."

Her eyes flared at his vow. There was no need to pretend this was all just a nice friendship when it wasn't.

"When the case is over, are you just going to divorce me?" she asked. "I mean, I don't expect a commitment from you, but I know for me, this is getting more difficult. When I'm with you, I want…"

Nolan shouldn't have felt relieved, but he did. He didn't want her to finish that sentence. If Pepper was wanting more from him, what could he say? She was vulnerable right now and the last thing he wanted to do was hurt her.

"I want you," he told her matter-of-factly. "While we're married, I want you and only you. We're adults. We have a mutual passion. Why deny it?"

Pepper shook her head and let out a soft laugh. "You make things sound so simple when they obviously aren't."

"For now, we will make them simple." He added more fruit to her plate and a few slices of cheese. "Eat. Take care of that baby and yourself. Then we'll talk."

She quirked a brow. "Is that code for strip me naked and have your way with me?"

Damn if she wasn't sassy and so perfect. "That's exactly what it's code for. Now hurry up and eat."

They ate without speaking for a few minutes. Nothing awkward, just a comfortable silence, and he was thankful they were on the same page. He truly didn't want to cause her any more grief, but he also wanted her to know exactly where he stood.

"Tell me about Hayes. I know he's coming home, but I haven't seen him since I left."

Nolan peeled another piece of meat from his drumstick and popped it in his mouth. "Honestly, the last time he was home, he looked, I don't know, haunted.

I thought he was done with the military then, but he said he couldn't leave his men. Now, though, I worry something has happened. That he won't be the same guy we once knew."

Nolan hated that his younger brother had seen so much ugliness in this world. Hayes had a big heart—he wanted to save everyone and had been convinced he could make a difference. Nolan shared those same qualities, but he'd chosen a different path.

"I'm sorry," she said. "Hopefully, being back home on the ranch, surrounded by family, will help him."

Nolan nodded. "I sure as hell hope so. I worry how he and Dad will be when they see each other. We never know what type of day Dad will be having and we won't know Hayes's frame of mind. They've both changed drastically over the past few years."

"Maybe they need each other," she replied, hope lacing her tone. "Sometimes one broken person just needs another to forge a new bond and become renewed."

Nolan considered her statement. As a doctor, he'd seen that exact thing happen between family members and friends. But when the circumstance involved his family, he wasn't so quick to believe it. A part of him knew, from a medical standpoint, that his father wasn't going to be cured. He was a prisoner in his own mind, and Nolan wasn't sure Hayes would be much better.

"I just want Hayes to understand that he can talk to us when he gets home, but he's the most stubborn of all the Elliott boys." Nolan paused to eat a grape.

"I wish he had someone in his life. He doesn't need to be alone with his thoughts every night. At least with Colt moving forward with the dude-ranch plans, maybe Hayes will jump on board."

"He'll be fine," Pepper assured him. "He has a great support team here. If he wants to talk, he will. Just don't crowd him and don't treat him like you're afraid he'll break."

Nolan stared into her dark eyes. For a woman who'd had hurdle after hurdle placed in front of her, she was surprisingly optimistic. She was always optimistic, always proving that life wasn't going to get the better of her. He sincerely hoped she and Hayes could talk.

"You're pretty remarkable," he murmured. "I've always known it, but I guess I didn't realize just how determined you are to see the bright side of everything."

Pepper shrugged. "There's not many options but to move forward, are there? I mean, it would be easy to lie around and feel sorry for yourself or think of all that has gone wrong in your life, but that won't accomplish much and you'll only feel worse. I admit, though, when I left here, I was so depressed. I'd lost a baby, lost you. My entire future, my dreams were just…gone."

Pepper glanced down at her swollen belly. "I wasn't sure I could move on, but then I knew if I ever did have a child, I certainly wouldn't tell them to ever give up."

When she looked back up to him, she offered a

sweet smile. "Hayes will be fine. He'll take time to adjust, but I'm confident you all will be just fine. Perhaps wait until your dad is having a better day to take Hayes to see him."

Nolan nodded. "I'm going to check with the facility. I want to bring Dad here for a day, but only if we're all in agreement that he'll be fine once we're here. I don't want to confuse him even more."

When she reached across and gripped his hand, Nolan stilled. She'd never initiated any contact since they'd been married.

"You know, when I left, I was convinced you didn't have a heart." She squeezed his hand. "I hated you for making me fall in love with you. I see now that fear drives you. You were afraid of being a father, of being with me and raising a family. You're afraid of your brother coming home because you're worried about getting entangled in his living nightmare."

Nolan had no idea how she'd managed to dissect him so perfectly when he'd never once thought that about himself. But she was dead-on. He *was* afraid. Staying detached was the best way to avoid those damn emotions.

"You're a great doctor because you care," she went on. "But you can keep your heart at a distance because you don't know the patients personally."

Nolan flipped his hand over and laced their fingers together. "Don't start analyzing me, babe. I'm not the man you used to know."

She tipped her head back and those gray eyes

seemed to penetrate straight through to his heart. Damn it. No. His heart wasn't involved. It wasn't.

"You're not the same man," she agreed. "You've put these walls up that weren't there when we were together before. It's almost as if..."

He cringed, gripped her hand even tighter as he watched the truth dawn in her eyes. But he didn't look away, as much as he wanted to. He held her gaze, willing her to say nothing, knowing she'd reveal exactly what had happened to him. She was too smart, too in tune with him even after all this time.

"What happened to you when I left?" she whispered, tears filling her eyes.

Oh, no. He wasn't going to get into this.

Nolan started to release her hand, but she squeezed and held him in place. "Nolan. Before I told you I was pregnant, we were so happy, so perfect. Then the miscarriage tore us apart. You started changing before my eyes. You're hardened now," she added with a slight shake of her head. "It's like you refused to let anyone in after I was gone."

That was exactly what happened, but he sure as hell wasn't about to keep going with this prodding. There were more interesting things he wanted to do tonight, and other plans he had for that mouth of hers.

"I thought you were tired," he stated, coming to his feet. He reached down for her hands and tugged her up and against his chest, pleased when her eyes widened. "You seem wide-awake now."

Her rounded belly between them had become so familiar. This might not be his child, but he loved seeing how Pepper's body transformed. She was even more vibrant and sexier than ever.

Nolan slid one hand on the side of her abdomen. "How are you feeling? Be honest. I'm a doctor, I know when people are lying."

She covered his hand with her own. "I feel great. I obviously needed to eat something."

"No more problems?" he asked.

Pepper shook her head. "None. I promise to tell you if anything at all happens."

Nolan picked her up once again with his arm behind her knees and the other supporting her back. "Time for bed."

Her laugh sent a jolt of arousal pumping through him…as if he needed another reason to want her.

"I'm not tired anymore," she stated, throwing her arms around his neck.

Nolan paused at the base of the steps and looked her in the eyes. "I don't plan on sleeping."

Her gaze dropped to his mouth and Nolan took off up the stairs. If she kept looking at him like that, he'd take her right in the hallway, and she deserved a bed. He might desire her with a need even greater than he could comprehend, but he wasn't going to be a complete savage. He'd already taken her on his couch among packages. It was time to step up his game.

Only this wasn't a game. This was Pepper. The only women who'd ever truly held a piece of his heart. The only woman he'd ever temporarily marry to get her out of a bind.

"Are you doing this because I was getting too close

to figuring you out?" she asked softly, laying her head on his shoulder.

"I planned on seducing you anyway. Your analysis of me may have accelerated the plans a bit."

Her fingertips slid through the hair on the nape of his neck. Just the slightest touch from her could get his body stirring. There was something so incredibly special about Pepper, beyond their past. She was…

No. Now was not the time to get into his head. He had a sexy woman ensconced in his arms and he'd just stepped over the threshold to his bedroom…*their* bedroom.

"We still need to talk," she informed him. "But it can wait."

Nolan smiled triumphantly as he made his way toward his king-size bed. Carefully, he laid her on top of the duvet and looked down at her. Something twisted inside his chest, something he refused to take the time to identify.

But seeing her in his bed, all spread out and her body lush from her pregnancy, Nolan knew he wasn't in such a hurry for this marriage to end. He rather liked seeing her in his bed.

Pepper extended her arms. "I've wanted to be here…with you…ever since I moved in."

"You denied it." He started ripping off his clothes, his ego boosted just a bit more when her eyes raked over his bare chest.

"I didn't want to let myself feel." Raising herself up on her elbows, she stared at him through those heavy lids. "You understand all about guarding your heart, don't you?"

Enough talk. Nolan reached for the elastic waist of her long skirt and yanked it down her smooth legs. Before he could reach for the hem of her tank, she'd already whipped it up and over her head and tossed it to the floor.

With Pepper in only her simple white bra and panties, Nolan took in her perfect body. Placing a knee on the bed, he put a hand on either side of her face and leaned down to nip playfully at her lips.

"You won't sleep anywhere else," he commanded. "This is your bed as long as you're here."

"I don't want to be anywhere else."

He took his time peeling off the rest of her clothes. The turmoil swirling around inside him had no place in this moment. Whatever doubts he had, any fears or unknowns, would not join them in this bed. Their marriage was one big question mark as far as the future, but the end was coming. And he wasn't quite ready to say goodbye just yet.

When he joined their bodies, Nolan made the mistake of gazing straight down into her eyes. There was no denying the emotions staring right back up at him. A heady feeling he recognized all too well. But the pressure of what that entailed wasn't something he was ready to face right now.

Nolan closed his eyes and slid his lips over hers. As he started to move, she clutched at his shoulders and kissed him with so much passion and, damn it, love that he was having a difficult time differentiating his own deeper feelings from the physical ones.

He tried to focus on her tiny whimpers, her warm breath on his shoulder. He made sure to balance his weight on his forearms beside her head, keeping most of his torso off hers.

The moment her body tightened all around him, Nolan increased the pace and kissed her one last time as he followed her over the edge.

For now, she was in his bed…but soon that would come to an end. Then he'd move on just like he'd always wanted. The unwelcome pang in his chest irritated him. He'd made his decision and he was happy.

Damn it. He wasn't going to revisit the past.

Nolan wrapped Pepper in his arms and rolled to his side, tucking her firmly against him. Stick with the plan, he reminded himself. When this case was all over and Pepper was back in her newly renovated apartment, Nolan would return to that perfect life that suited him so well.

Then something shifted inside him as he protectively rested his palm over his wife's belly. How many times could he tell himself he was happy alone until he finally believed it?

Seventeen

Pepper had just unlocked the back door to her shop when her cell rang. She juggled her purse, her small lunch bag, and her cell, all while trying to turn the key and not drop anything.

"Hello," she finally managed after pushing the door open.

"Pepper, I have some news."

She closed the door behind her as the attorney's words gave her heart a mild attack. "Is something wrong? I thought we were meeting later this week."

"That won't be necessary anymore," he informed her. "The Wrights' attorney called and they've decided to drop the case."

Pepper's knees nearly gave out. She crossed the

back room to put her stuff on her worktable before sinking down into her old metal chair.

"What? Why? I mean, I'm thankful, but what caused the sudden change?"

"Money talks and they needed it. They'd like you to consider letting them see the baby, but they've given up the idea of custody. They've been well compensated."

Nolan. There was no other way to explain it. He'd done this. She didn't even need to ask. He'd done so much for her and he was making sure she had the life she'd always wanted.

Pepper absolutely hated that her child had been basically used by the Wrights for less-than-altruistic reasons. But if they were that quick to drop the case over money, then they weren't fit to be guardians and raise her child anyway.

Relief swept over her. Pepper rested a hand on her belly just as her little guy started to kick. Tears pricked her eyes, but she swallowed back the emotions. She didn't want to break down over the phone.

"Have you told Nolan they officially dropped the case?" she asked.

"I wanted to tell you first."

Pepper drew in a deep breath. "Okay, then. I'll call him. But first I have to thank you. It sounds so simple and not nearly adequate enough, but you don't know how much I appreciate what you did."

"It was my pleasure," he told her with a smile to his voice. "But if you want to thank anyone, that would be Nolan. He was checking in with me constantly, following up with the investigator, making sure we knew to stop at nothing, and to put your case first."

Pepper's heart flipped. She'd made love to her husband every night for the past five nights. She'd not once told him her feelings had evolved into something so much more than she'd ever thought possible. And now hearing just how diligent he'd been in getting this case dropped, she knew for a fact she'd fallen in love with him all over again.

No, not again. What she felt now was so much more intense than what she had before. And if she was honest, she'd have to admit she never stopped loving him. All the hurt she'd built up had just pushed that love to the back of her mind, but it was always there, just waiting to be given new life.

"Well, I still want to thank you," she reiterated. "I'll call Nolan right now."

"Congratulations," he told her before they disconnected the call.

Pepper got to her feet, suddenly feeling lighter than she had in weeks. Then a sense of melancholy washed over her. She'd been Mrs. Nolan Elliott for less than a month and it was already coming to an end.

She glanced down at the ring that had been his mother's. Pepper didn't want to take it off, didn't want to put this chapter behind her. She wanted to write the rest of their story and she wanted Nolan in her life permanently and for real.

But he'd made it clear they were over once the custody battle was resolved. Was that why he'd been so forceful with his lawyer and investigator? Was he that eager to get back to his old lifestyle? He'd been all too anxious to have her gone before—maybe he missed having his house all to himself.

Pepper started to call him when the back door swung open. She spun around, clutching her cell to her chest.

"I'm sorry." The contractor stared back at her, holding his hands up. "I didn't mean to startle you."

"Oh, it's okay. What can I help you with?"

"I just wanted to let you know that we should be finishing up today. We're just putting the trim back in place and cleaning up our mess and we should be gone by this afternoon."

Pepper blinked. "So, I can move back in?"

He nodded. "Yes, ma'am."

She swallowed a lump in her throat as her heart clenched. Her time at Pebblebrook really was coming to an abrupt halt. That was what she wanted, wasn't it? She wanted to get back into her apartment and start setting up for her baby. That had been the goal all along.

"Thank you," she told him, forcing a smile. "I'll let Nolan know and make sure he gets with you so you can be paid."

He waved a hand to dismiss her. "Mr. Elliott has already paid us enough. It's all covered."

The contractor left just as abruptly as he came and Pepper was left feeling such a mixture of emotions. She should have been elated that this time had come, but all she felt was that grip on her secret desires starting to slip once again. She'd been holding on to that dream, the dream she'd had years ago. Since she came back to Stone River, she hadn't realized she'd reached for it again, but she had…with both hands this time.

She wanted to continue to be Mrs. Elliott. She wanted to raise her child at Pebblebrook, and she wanted those things with Nolan as a loving spouse and parent.

If she thought he was even interested, then she'd fight for what she wanted. But he had done all of this only out of guilt, and out of primal attraction. That clearly wasn't enough to build a life on.

Pepper figured all of this needed to be done face-to-face. She'd wait until the end of the day and then go home. Hayes was coming back to the ranch today, so Nolan would be occupied. Then she could think of what to say.

How did she thank him or pay him back for such a sacrifice? How did she even find the right words for a goodbye such as this? Nothing about their reunion had been normal. She wanted to let him know how much she truly appreciated his help, but nothing was coming to mind…basically because she'd fallen in love with him again.

Pepper shook off her own heartache and decided to push forward. After all, she'd secured her son's future and that was all that had mattered since the beginning.

Nolan had been waiting on the front porch of Hayes's house for the past hour. Over the last several nights he'd grown even closer with Pepper. Their lovemaking had been so much more than just physical. They'd shared an intimacy that seemed to be intensifying, and there wasn't much he could do to stop it.

She'd woken him in the middle of the night to feel her son kick, and they'd ended up down in the kitchen for a snack…then he'd taken her right on the kitchen island.

Nolan crossed his ankles in front of him and rested his arms on the rocker. He and Pepper had settled into a dynamic of playing house so flawlessly he would swear she wasn't acting…and he wasn't so sure he was, either.

As the sound of Colt's truck rumbled nearby, Nolan came to his feet. The truck rounded the last bend and Nolan was off the porch and heading toward the drive. He couldn't wait to see his brother again.

Colt's truck came to a stop and Nolan crossed to the passenger side. Hayes's door flung open and his brother stepped out in his BDUs and combat boots. His military-short hair only accentuated his eyes. The light wasn't there like it had been when they were younger.

"Hey, man." Nolan wrapped both arms around his brother and gave him a hard slap on the back before stepping away. "Good to see you."

Hayes nodded. "Good to be home."

Colt came around the truck and shot Nolan a look. Nolan wasn't sure what silent code he was trying to convey, but they'd definitely talk later in private.

"Your kitchen is stocked," Colt stated. "And I had

some of my guys make sure everything was working fine. Water, electric. The air-conditioning has been on for a day to cool things off and you're good to go."

Hayes nodded and glanced around the portion of the property that belonged to him. His home had been the original house on Pebblebrook. Their grandfather had built it and their father had grown up there. Now with Colt and Nolan having their own homes on the spread, Hayes kept this one for himself.

And Colt's twin, Beau, was still out in Hollywood driving women crazy with his looks and making millions flashing his dimples and Southern charm on the screen. He rarely came home and when he did, he didn't spend more than a few days at a time.

"I missed this smell," Hayes said quietly.

"Manure?" Colt asked with a laugh. "We can put you right to work whenever you're up to it."

Hayes shoved his hands in his pockets and rocked back on his heels. "The sooner, the better. I'm not used to idle time."

Just as Nolan figured. His brother was going to have to stay busy. There was always plenty to do on a farm, so that was no problem. The real problem was that haunted look in his younger brother's eyes.

"Well, the dude-ranch plans are coming along," Colt said. "The engineer has finalized the plans and we're going to be building a few cabins back on the east side of the property."

"Dad would love that," Hayes replied before inhaling deeply and turning to Nolan. "How is he?"

Nolan released a breath. He wasn't going to sugarcoat things—Hayes would learn for himself soon enough. "He's not having as many good days as he used to. He's in the past more often than not and wants to know why mom isn't there. He fell the other night, but thankfully, nothing was broken."

"I want to see him."

"Of course. Do you want one of us to go with you?" Colt asked, tipping his hat to shield his face from the sun.

Hayes shook his head. "That's not necessary. I don't need you all hovering over me now that I'm home. I just need to get readjusted. It will take some time."

Nolan met Colt's gaze.

"Stop it," Hayes demanded. "I see the looks you two are throwing back and forth. Yeah, I'm not the same guy I was before I went over to that hellhole, but I'm still your brother and I'm still a rancher."

"We worry," Colt stated gruffly.

Hayes let out a dry, humorless laugh. "That makes three of us, but I'm okay. Well, I'm not exactly okay, but I'll be fine. Just…don't crowd me. Okay?"

Nolan and Colt nodded, but Nolan also knew there was no way they were going to let their brother deal with this darkness on his own. They might all be living their own lives, going their own ways, but they were still family and that was all that mattered.

"Just tell us what you need," Colt replied. "This is new for us, too, so we want to help but we don't want to make this more difficult, either."

Hayes nodded and reached into the truck for his

bag. His government-issued bag that had traveled through hell and back with him. Nolan watched as Hayes flung the large army-green sack over his shoulder and headed toward his house.

Colt shut the truck door and leaned back against it. "One of us needs to check on him pretty often until we see exactly what we're dealing with."

Nolan took off his hat and swiped the sweat from his forehead. "He'll be pissed if he thinks we're babysitting."

"I don't care what he thinks," Colt retorted. "It's better than having him suffer alone or worse. You know all those horror stories of soldiers who came home and couldn't handle the civilian life."

"Maybe seeing Dad will help him," Nolan said, propping his hat back on his head. "Dad may not know who he is, but this may be a simple case where Hayes will see someone is also struggling with identity. Or Dad may shock us and know exactly who Hayes is."

"I sure as hell hope so," Colt muttered.

His thoughts exactly. Nolan wasn't sure how these next few days, weeks or even months would play out, but he had to be aware of everything where his brother was concerned.

And not just his brother, but his wife. There were so many uncertainties with her, with their future. All he knew was he loved having her in his home, in his bed. He'd not wanted marriage, a family. But she'd come back into his life and thrust every bit of that into his face. He needed her, wanted her and planned on having her. Permanently.

"I have to go," he told Colt. "I need to get home."

Nolan hopped on his four-wheeler and headed for his house, ready to talk to Pepper.

Eighteen

Nolan came to an abrupt halt at the threshold of his bedroom. Lying out on the bed was a suitcase, clothes haphazardly piled all over it.

Pepper came out of the adjoining bath clutching her toiletry bag. As soon as her eyes locked on to his, she froze.

"I didn't know you were back." She worried her bottom lip as she held his gaze. "Um, how's Hayes?"

Nolan took one careful step in, as if any abrupt movement would shatter this already-fragile situation. "He's okay. Or he will be with time."

When she nodded and put her small bag on top of her existing pile, Nolan shook his head. "Care to tell me what's going on?"

Pepper turned, smoothing her hand over her fitted

tank. "I have quite a bit of news, actually. The case was dropped, thanks to you and your investigator."

Surprised, Nolan smiled. "That's great news. Seems rather abrupt, though."

"Your money and power talked louder than I could, so I'm indebted to you." She crossed her arms over her chest and tilted her head. "The contractor finished up this afternoon, so my apartment is all ready for me. Looks like everything fell into place just when I needed it to."

When she needed it to. Those words were like a dagger straight to his heart…the heart he hadn't wanted to get involved in this marriage.

"You don't owe me anything," he managed after a moment. "You don't have to rush out, though."

Damn it, he didn't want her to leave at all, but apparently she couldn't get away from him fast enough.

"We agreed when the case was over, there was no need to be married." Pepper drew in a deep breath and dropped her arms, her bangle bracelets jingling. He'd become so used to hearing that sound he found even that simple gesture was something he'd miss. "I'm not going to drag this out any longer. We both have lives we need to get on with. I'm borrowing one of your suitcases since the clothes were here already. I'll pay you back for those, as well, once I get a solid income going. I'll let you contact your attorney regarding the divorce."

The divorce. Why were her parting words so damn soul crushing? He'd wanted this. He'd laid out the guidelines from the beginning. He'd just thought he'd have more time. This all seemed so sudden—there was no transition period. She was in his bed last night, all wrapped around him, and now she was hell-bent on making tracks to get out. And she'd laid out her speech so nice and neat as if she'd spent the past few hours rehearsing it. Was that so she could deliver it void of all emotion? If so, she'd nailed it.

"Sure," he muttered. "I can do that."

Her eyes darted back to her suitcase, then to him. "If you don't mind, can you start loading my car with all the baby stuff we bought? Then I can get this."

He swallowed, hating how she seemed to be so distant and almost cold. His Pepper had always been so forthcoming with her feelings, but now, well, she had erected some wall between them that hadn't existed before. She was done—that much was evident.

Could she seriously just leave without caring? He desperately wanted to know what she was thinking. But from the hasty way she was tossing things into her suitcase—*his* suitcase—perhaps it was best he didn't know.

"I'll bring the baby stuff later," he told her. "Just concentrate on your things for now."

"Oh, right. Of course." She turned to the bed and quickly held the suitcase zipper together and forced it shut. "I'll be in the shop tomorrow if you want to come by then and drop it off."

She tugged the suitcase off the bed.

"Damn it, let me get that." He crossed the room and jerked the luggage from her hand.

"Why are you so angry?" she asked, looking up

at him with those big, expressive eyes. "We agreed to this, and I can't stay here forever. You and I both know we have lives to get back to, and our time of playing house wasn't meant to be long-term."

Nolan hated how she tossed his own words back into his face. He hated that she was right because they were different people with different goals. Yet, somehow over these past couple of weeks, that line he didn't want to cross had become blurred. So blurred he had no idea where it even was anymore.

"This doesn't have to be difficult," she whispered. "You're off the hook. I mean, we're legally still married, but I don't expect you to remain faithful to me."

Her eyes darted away, but her words said everything. She was giving him permission to move on with another woman...and if that didn't speak volumes for where she stood, the loaded suitcase in his hand sure as hell did.

Nolan stepped aside and let her pass. "I'll take this down for you."

Pepper met his gaze once more. Biting her lip again, she nodded and eased by. As he watched her retreating back, he realized she'd never be in this room again. They'd never share a bed or late-night snacks in his kitchen. He wouldn't roll over in the middle of the night and feel her son kick.

Nolan swallowed hard and pulled the luggage behind him as he headed for the stairs. He'd never begged a woman to stay and he certainly wasn't going to start now. If Pepper wanted to go, then he had to set her free. He'd be fine—after all, he'd moved on the last time she walked out of his life.

But this time seemed so different, so final. And his heart hadn't felt this empty the last time.

She wasn't even officially gone and his house already had a void that he knew would never be filled.

Pepper left her suitcase in the car. She didn't care about her clothes, her toothbrush, her underwear. None of that mattered when her heart was in shattered pieces.

Nolan hadn't asked her to stay. He'd told her she didn't have to be in a rush, but he hadn't told her he wanted her in his home, in his life…his heart. Pepper had prayed he'd come home, pull her into his arms, and tell her he wanted her to stay. Convince her that the case and her apartment didn't matter. She desperately wanted him to tell her that her only home was with him at Pebblebrook.

But he hadn't and she had too much pride to open up about her true feelings. She'd been burned before by this man. The only problem now was the flame was still burning.

Pepper walked around her newly renovated apartment and toyed with the ring still mocking her on her finger. She'd forgotten to return it, but she couldn't bring herself to take it off just yet. The marriage was over, but…maybe she could hang on in private just a bit longer.

The faint smell of wood and paint had her making a mental note to pick up some potpourri tomorrow. The laminate floor that stretched from the living room through the open kitchen and on into the bedrooms was perfect. She was so glad all the flooring was new. She'd find some bright rugs to put down and…

Tears filled her eyes as she covered her face and let the dam burst. She didn't care about rugs or flooring or anything else right now. She already missed Pebblebrook. In such a short time she'd made that place her home. She'd tried to remain detached, but how could she when she'd been staying in the home she'd helped design with the man she'd never stopped loving?

Now that she was alone, she planned on taking the rest of the evening for a good cry. The kind of cry that made the tip of her nose red, her skin splotchy, her eyes puffy. She'd just have to use extra concealer tomorrow for work.

Pepper headed to her fridge and realized with a pang of dismay that there was no food. Her new kitchen was perfect with the tiled backsplash and quartz countertops…but there was no emergency stash of ice cream in the freezer.

There was no way she was in the mood to go back out. It was getting late, not terribly so, but she'd had a rough day and she was emotionally drained.

Only another woman would understand this type of need. It wasn't as if Pepper had made a bunch of friends since she'd been back. She'd been busy with her shop, busy dodging custody issues and busy getting married to the one man she loved but who didn't love her in return.

If only there were some reality show on screwing up your life in epic proportions.

Pepper grabbed her phone from her purse and shot off a text. There was one other woman who might actually know what Pepper was going through. Annabelle was the closest thing she had to a friend and she knew all about those Elliott boys. Annabelle had gone into all the mayhem that had surrounded her relationship with Colt. That woman definitely understood a frustrating, arrogant, sexy cowboy.

Pepper wasn't even sure if she wanted to talk about this—everything was still so fresh, so raw. But perhaps Annabelle could just leave a copious amount of ice cream on the stoop outside the apartment door and go.

In the bottom of her bag, Pepper found a packet of pretzels and a bottle of water. Better than nothing, but she was going to need real food. Hopefully, Annabelle would take pity on her and bring a pizza or something with that ice cream. If there was ever a time that called for junk, it was now.

Pepper waited for the reply, hoping Colt's fiancée would come through. Because the only other person Pepper had leaned on was now out of her life…and filing for divorce.

Nineteen

Four days had passed since she left. Nolan had gone back to work on the second day and had been there since. What was the point in going home? Colt had promised to check on Hayes while Nolan was at the hospital. The surgeries had been brutal on him— one right after another. He was more than ready to get home and have the next two days off because he planned on sleeping and then diving into ranch work with his brothers.

But on his way home earlier, he'd come across an accident. After working thirty-six hours, he was dead on his feet and wanted nothing more than to fall face-first in his bed…or a guest bed since he couldn't bring himself to sleep where the sheets still smelled like his wife.

The second he'd become a doctor, he'd sworn to help those in need and there was a definite need at the accident site. A woman was in full-blown labor and her husband had been in a hurry to get her to the hospital and run a red light, and their car had been hit in the side.

Nolan had helped deliver the baby girl while waiting on the ambulance. He'd held the mother's hand as they'd loaded her into the back, but he could tell that she probably wasn't going to make it.

The harsh reality of that entire scene gnawed at his gut and he nearly felt sick. When the father held on to his precious baby while praying for his wife to live, Nolan had known that man wouldn't get a second chance.

But maybe Nolan could. Hell, he'd had his second chance and he'd blown it. He'd let Pepper walk out of his house and he hadn't put up a fight. Why? Because of his stupid pride and hardheaded mentality. So what if she laughed in his face or told him there was no way she'd stay married to a man who was a workaholic? He hadn't even tried to convince her to stay. Since when did he just give up on things?

Risking grief and heartache was completely worth it if the ultimate ending was joy and a life with Pepper. He wanted all they could have, all they'd lost. They were both getting a second chance and he refused to walk away again.

As he headed to the kitchen to get a bottle of water, the ultrasound image of Pepper's son was the only thing stuck on the fridge door. Nolan slid his fingertip over the image and wondered if she'd left this for him on purpose to drive him out of his mind or if she'd legitimately forgot it in her haste to get out.

He grabbed the bottle and started to head upstairs to the shower. The piles of baby items in the living room caught his attention, though. All of the various things they'd shopped for. She'd been so excited that day, and he had to admit he'd had a great time watching her gather so many necessities for her son. He still needed to deliver all of that to her apartment, but he honestly had no idea how everything would fit in her living space. But it would all fit here in his home and he had plenty of bedrooms to spare for a nursery.

Pepper and the baby were so much more important than this ranch or his MD, and he'd fought like hell to make both of those top priority in his life.

Nolan wanted to call the hospital and check on the patient, but in his heart he already knew the outcome. Plus, if he didn't check in, then there was still that glimmer of hope that she'd pulled through.

And there was a glimmer of hope that he and Pepper could pull through, too. He just had to man up and go to her. He'd make her listen to what he had to say, to the reasons they should be together. If she chose to push him away, then he could live with it. He'd hate it, but at least he'd know he did all he could to get her to come back where she belonged...right here at Pebblebrook.

If Hayes was looking for a second chance at life after all he'd been through, why the hell couldn't

Nolan? The only person standing in the way of what he wanted was himself.

Nolan was going to fight for his wife.

Pepper brushed the navy strokes over her stark white canvas. Once she had the background, she planned on free-handing a quote with her son's name. She'd opted to push forward with her thoughts, even if her heart hadn't quite caught up yet. So the past few days she'd devoted to all things baby and she'd finally come up with a name.

She touched up the edges, making sure all the white was covered, and took a step back to examine the even strokes. Someone pounded on her door, making Pepper jump and swipe the brush across her cheek.

With a groan, she dropped the brush into the cup of water and wiped her hands on the towel before heading to the door. She'd deal with her cheek in a bit.

Her heart kicked up because she figured there was only one person who could be on the other side of that door. She assumed Nolan was finally delivering that baby stuff. Seeing him would hurt, but she was going to have to get used to it. They lived in the same town now and running into him was inevitable.

Drawing a steadying breath, Pepper glanced through the peephole. Her eyes immediately landed on his dark, disheveled hair. He'd turned his back and those broad shoulders were encased in a formfitting tee that made her remember exactly what those hard-packed muscles had felt like beneath her hands.

Rubbing her fingers together, she took another breath before flicking the lock open. Nolan turned as she swung the door open.

"If you have the baby's things—"

"I don't." He moved into the doorway, crowding her until she backed up. "I came to talk to you. You don't have to say anything. Just give me five minutes."

He didn't give her a chance to reply as he skirted around her. Realizing she didn't have much choice, Pepper closed the door. Whatever he wanted, she prayed he made it fast. Five minutes with Nolan was cruel when she knew he didn't reciprocate her feelings. And if he hadn't brought the baby things, what did he want?

Crossing her arms, Pepper spun around and remained in place. Nolan was at the art table she'd set up in the living area. He stared at the navy canvas, then looked back to her.

"What's this going to be?" he asked.

"For the nursery." When he continued to stare, Pepper let out a sigh and threw her arms wide. "If you came for small talk, I'm busy."

Nolan raked a hand over his jawline, the stubble scraping beneath his palm. She finally took a moment to study his appearance. His eyes were puffy and dark, as if sleep had not been his friend for quite some time. The finger marks through his hair were evidence of his frustrated state. Yet she didn't feel sorry for him. He could've had everything—she would've given him everything—in exchange for love. Was that too much to ask?

"What do you want, Nolan? Because you look like you're about to keel over."

He met her gaze across the narrow space. "My thirty-six-hour shift ended a few hours ago. I was caught behind a wreck and delivered a baby. I managed to run home and shower before coming here because I was a total mess."

Pepper gasped and took a step toward him. "Why on earth aren't you in bed? How's the baby? Did you have to deliver in the car?"

She couldn't help firing off questions, because she had so many, but most of all she wanted to know why he was here when it was obvious he was a zombie.

"The baby is fine. I delivered a healthy baby girl on the side of the highway while we waited on paramedics." Nolan shook his head and glanced down to his cowboy boots. "I'm almost positive the mother didn't make it, though. I couldn't call and find out. I just… I didn't want to know."

Pepper's heart clenched. She fisted her hands at her sides and waited for him to continue. Maybe he'd come because he just needed someone to talk to. If that was the case, she'd listen. She loved him too much to turn him away, even if he didn't love her in return.

"I've been a doctor for years," he went on as he brought his haunted eyes back up to hers. "I try not to get emotionally attached, but this case…"

The pregnant woman. The possible loss of life.

It was all making sense now. Pepper slowly took a step forward, then another. Dare she hope he'd had some epiphany? While her heart literally ached for the family of the woman who'd just delivered, if that instance brought Nolan to her door, back into her life, she had to believe he was at that scene for a reason.

Nolan watched her as she neared. When she came toe-to-toe with him, he reached for her arms and pulled her close.

"Not everybody gets a second chance," he whispered into her hair. Pepper trembled as she wrapped her arms around him. "I don't deserve a second chance, but I let you walk out of my life once. Then you walked out of my house. I can't let you go, Pepper."

Instant joy and relief flooded through her as she gripped his shirt and rested her forehead against his chest. "Are you here to ask me to come back?"

Nolan eased away but kept his grip on her. "I'm telling you that my life has been empty since you left ten years ago. I'm telling you that Pebblebrook is lonely and everywhere I look in my house I see you. The paintings, the ultrasound image you left. There's even a pair of flip-flops by my back door. They're waiting on you, Pepper. I'm waiting on you. Come home."

Pepper's eyes burned as tears welled up. "Why?" she couldn't help but ask. "Why do you want me to come back? I'm pregnant with another man's baby, our marriage was a farce, and—"

"I love you."

Those three simple yet life-changing words had her stilling. "You...love me?"

He framed her face in his large hands, swiping the blue paint from her cheek with the pad of his thumb. When he held it up in front of her face, he smiled.

"I love this. I love the free spirit inside of you. I love the creativity you have to make something from nothing." He took the blue and wiped it on his own cheek. "Make a life with me, Pepper. Make something from nothing with this heart of mine."

Oh, that did it. She sobbed, falling into his chest as her emotions completely overtook her.

Nolan's arms enveloped her as he smoothed her hair down her back. "I was hoping for a better response," he rasped.

Pepper laughed through the tears. "I just wanted you to love me as I love you. I had no idea you'd be so eloquent and perfect when you told me."

"I should've told you long ago." He leaned back and brushed his mouth tenderly over hers before pulling away. "This marriage isn't a farce. It's very real and it's forever. Come back to Pebblebrook. I'll give you all the babies you want and I'll raise this son as my own."

Pepper nodded, letting out a hiccup with her tears. "I'm a mess," she muttered. "I didn't expect you to do this. I dreamed of it. I'd hoped you'd come to see that we deserve this second chance, but I really thought you'd pushed me out forever."

"I'm a fool for letting you go. I'll never make that mistake again." He kissed her hard, a promise of a lifetime together poured into that kiss. "Come home and we'll make a nursery and an art studio. We'll make the life we deserve. Together."

Pepper smiled and returned the kiss. "Together."

Epilogue

Hayes stared at the bottle of bourbon. He'd pulled out the unopened bottle from his cellar and had been eyeing the damn thing for the past hour.

Drinking would be the easy part. Getting lost in that bottle would be the coward's way out. But he wanted anything to dull the ache in his chest of being home. He'd known coming back would be difficult, but he hadn't expected the guilt that came along with being back at Pebblebrook.

He had all the money a man could ever want. He had a five-thousand-acre ranch, so work would definitely keep him busy. And he loved it here…but he'd left so many of his brothers overseas.

Hayes shut his eyes and tried to push his demons aside, but nothing helped. When he had his eyes open, all he saw was the life he had here in Stone River. The perfect life, some would call it. Money, power, family. Yes, he did have it all on a certain level.

He'd give it all up if he thought he could save his friends on the other side of the globe. Hayes grabbed the bottle and headed out onto the back porch. He'd inherited the original Elliott homestead and he loved this old two-story farmhouse. There was some work to be done, but he was ready to dive into a project that would keep his hands busy and his mind occupied.

Hayes sank into one of the old rockers on his porch. Clutching the bottle like some warped sense of a lifeline, he stared out at the darkened sky. There was nothing as peaceful as Pebblebrook. With a river running along the back of the property behind his house and a brook running through the front of the property where Colt's house was, there was so much beauty and tranquility here.

Quite the polar opposite of where he'd spent the last several years of his life. Coming home every twelve to eighteen months for a brief time wasn't the same as coming home for good. Other than farm life, what else did he know? What else did he do? Because with the way his heart and soul had been battered, he figured it best if he stayed on the ranch as much as possible until he got acclimated to civilian life again.

Colt and Nolan had both found love. Nolan and Pepper were married and blissfully in love. Both of his brothers seemed so happy. There must be something in the water because both of his brothers were going into ready-made families. Hayes wanted no part of kids. Hell, he wasn't even sure he could handle a regular relationship with a woman, let alone a child. He had too much darkness inside him, had seen too much to be a father.

But Colt had always wanted that large-family lifestyle, and Nolan had finally come to his senses where Pepper was concerned. Who knew love could last across a decade and time apart?

Hayes had no sweethearts in his past. He didn't do relationships because he'd been in the service and always traveling. Hell, he'd been married to the army, and just because he was getting out, didn't mean that he could simply turn off his feelings about the life he'd lived.

The bottle in his hand mocked him and he wanted to throw it to get rid of the temptation. He didn't know how long he sat and rocked, replaying his career in slow motion in his mind. A muscle ticked in his jaw. He knew his brothers were worried about him, and they had every right. But he meant what he said when he told them he needed space. If they started hovering, he wasn't sure he wouldn't lash out at them— and they were the last people on earth he wanted to get angry with.

Tomorrow he'd go see his father. He wasn't sure he'd be strong enough to see his formerly robust, vibrant father now in a nursing home not even knowing his own name at times. Hayes didn't care, though. He wanted to be there, to sit by his dad's side and do absolutely nothing. Hayes wanted that simplicity.

Hayes knew his father would be proud of Colt for

pushing ahead with the dude ranch. Opening Pebble-brook to the public had been a dream of their father's for some time, but he'd never fully gone ahead with the plans. Then dementia had stolen everything and the project had gotten pushed to the back of everyone's mind.

Hayes didn't recall the last time he'd seen Beau, other than on the big screen. Now that he was home, he wondered when they'd have an old-fashioned Elliott gathering. Hayes wanted everyone together—he wanted to go back to that time when they all hung out in the stables talking about nothing and everything. When they'd drink beers late at night, go for early-morning rides to check the fence lines... Hell, he just wanted an existence that didn't involve fearing for your life every single day.

Hayes set the bottle on the porch and leaned forward on his elbows. Resting his head in his hands, he sent up a prayer. He'd done quite a bit of that recently. He wasn't sure if anyone heard his thoughts, but he figured it didn't hurt.

He was home. All that mattered was that he was here now and he was going to heal. With the help of his brothers and his soon-to-be sisters-in-law, he wouldn't be alone.

Maybe, over time, he'd get back into the realm of socializing and perhaps even dating, but he wasn't going to plan too far ahead. One day at a time: that was how he had to live.

He got to his feet, crossed to the railing and rested his hands on the wood beam. Tomorrow he'd start renovating his home.

Home. He liked the sound of that, even if he would live in this big house all by himself.

He was home and that was more than some of his comrades had. Hayes would be happy with the life he'd been given and he'd push forward. Alone…just like he wanted.

* * * * *

*Pick up these other sexy romances
from Jules Bennett!*

*TWIN SECRETS
TRAPPED WITH THE TYCOON
FROM FRIEND TO FAKE FIANCÉ
HOLIDAY BABY SCANDAL
THE HEIR'S UNEXPECTED BABY*

Available now from Harlequin Desire!

* * *

*If you're on Twitter, tell us what you think
of Harlequin Desire! #harlequindesire*

COMING NEXT MONTH FROM

HARLEQUIN *Desire*

Available July 3, 2017

#2527 THE BABY FAVOR
Billionaires and Babies • by Andrea Laurence
CEO Mason Spencer and his wife are headed for divorce when an old promise changes their plans. They are now the guardians for Spencer's niece...and they must remain married. Will this be their second chance, one that leads to forever?

#2528 LONE STAR BABY SCANDAL
Texas Cattleman's Club: Blackmail • by Lauren Canan
When sexy former rodeo champion turned billionaire Clay Everett sets his sights on his spunky secretary, he's sure he holds the reins in their affair. Until he learns Sophie Prescott is carrying his child. Now all bets are off!

#2529 HIS UNEXPECTED HEIR
Little Secrets • by Maureen Child
After a fling with a sexy marine leaves Rita pregnant, her attempts to reach the billionaire are met with silence...until now! Brooding, reclusive Jack offers to marry Rita—in name only. Will his new family give him the heart to embrace life—and love—again?

#2530 PREGNANT BY THE BILLIONAIRE
The Locke Legacy • by Karen Booth
Billionaire Sawyer Locke only makes commitments to his hotel empire—until he meets fiery PR exec Kendall Ross. Now he can't get her out of his mind—or out of his bed. But when she becomes pregnant, will he claim the heir he never expected?

#2531 BEST FRIEND BRIDE
In Name Only • by Kat Cantrell
CEO Jonas Kim must stop his arranged marriage—by arranging a marriage for himself! His best friend, Vivian, will be his wife and never fall in love, or so he thinks. Can he keep his heart safe when Viv tempts him to become friends with benefits?

#2532 CLAIMING THE COWGIRL'S BABY
Red Dirt Royalty • by Silver James
Rancher Kaden inherited a birth father, a powerful last name and wealth—none of which he wants. His pregnant lover, debutante Pippa Duncan, has lost everything due to a dark family secret. Their marriage of convenience may undo the pain of their families' pasts, but will it lead to love?

YOU CAN FIND MORE INFORMATION ON UPCOMING HARLEQUIN® TITLES, FREE EXCERPTS AND MORE AT WWW.HARLEQUIN.COM.

Get 2 Free Books,

◆ HARLEQUIN *Desire*

Plus 2 Free Gifts—

just for trying the Reader Service!

After a fling with a sexy marine leaves Rita pregnant, her attempts to reach the billionaire are met with silence…until now! Brooding, reclusive Jack offers to marry Rita—in name only. Will his new family give him the heart to embrace life—and love—again?

Read on for a sneak peek of
LITTLE SECRETS: HIS UNEXPECTED HEIR
by USA TODAY bestselling author Maureen Child.

Jack didn't make a habit of coming here. Memories were thick and he tended to avoid them, because remembering wouldn't get him a damn thing. But against his will, images filled his mind.

Every damn moment of that time with Rita was etched into his brain in living, vibrant color. He could hear the sound of her voice. The music of her laughter. He saw the shine in her eyes and felt the silk of her touch.

"And you've been working for months to forget it," he reminded himself in a mutter. "No point in dredging it up now."

What they'd found together all those months ago was over. There was no going back. He'd made a promise to himself. One he intended to keep.

It was a hard lesson to learn, but he had learned it in the hot, dry sands of a distant country. And that lesson haunted him to this day.

HDEXP0617

But Jack Buchanan didn't surrender to the dregs of fear, so he kept walking, made himself notice the everyday world pulsing around him. Along the street, a pair of musicians was playing for the crowd and the dollar bills tossed into an open guitar case. Shop owners had tables set up outside their storefronts to entice customers and, farther down the street, a line snaked from a bakery's doors all along the sidewalk.

He hadn't been downtown in months, so he'd never seen the bakery before. Apparently, though, it had quite the loyal customer base. Dozens of people—from teenagers to career men and women—waited patiently to get through the open bakery door. As he got closer, amazing scents wafted through the air and he understood the crowds gathering. Idly, Jack glanced through the wide, shining front window at the throng within, then stopped dead as an all-too-familiar laugh drifted to him.

Everything inside Jack went cold and still. He hadn't heard that laughter in months, but he'd have known it anywhere. Throaty, rich, it made him think of long hot nights, silk sheets and big brown eyes staring up into his in the darkness.

He'd tried to forget her. Had, he'd thought, buried the memories; yet now they came roaring back, swamping him until Jack had to fight for breath.

Even as he told himself it couldn't be her, Jack was bypassing the line and stalking into the bakery.

Don't miss
LITTLE SECRETS: HIS UNEXPECTED HEIR
by USA TODAY *bestselling author Maureen Child,*
available July 2017 wherever
Harlequin® Desire books and ebooks are sold.

www.Harlequin.com

HARLEQUIN® *Desire*

AVAILABLE JULY 2017
LONE STAR BABY SCANDAL
BY
LAUREN CANAN

PART OF THE SIZZLING
TEXAS CATTLEMAN'S CLUB: BLACKMAIL SERIES

When sexy former rodeo champion turned billionaire Clay Everett
sets his sights on his spunky secretary, he's sure he holds the reins
in their affair. Until he learns Sophie Prescott is carrying his child.
Now all bets are off!

AND DON'T MISS A SINGLE INSTALLMENT OF

TEXAS CATTLEMAN'S CLUB:
BLACKMAIL

No secret—or heart—is safe in Royal, Texas...

— www.Harlequin.com —

HD83855

HARLEQUIN®
A *Romance* FOR EVERY MOOD™

Love the Harlequin book you just read?

Your opinion matters.

Review this book on your favorite
book site, review site, blog or your own
social media properties and share
your opinion with other readers!

Turn your love of reading into rewards you'll love with
Harlequin My Rewards